GISELA'S PASSION

ASTRID V. J.

First edition November 2019

Editing by Qat Wanders
E detail designed by Theresia Schmid
Cover design by Emily's World of Design

ISBN 978-91-985519-4-5 (paperback)
ISBN 978-91-985519-5-2 (ebook)

Published by New Wings Press
Oluff Nilssonsvägen 10, Partille, Sweden

Dedicated in loving memory to
Maria Alexandra Lorenza Soledad and
to all the other dancers in my family

Theresa Jeanette
Ámbar Maya
Alexandra Chiara

SCATTERED THUNDER

This is the house that nobody comes to
Nobody comes to this house
This is the couch that nobody sits on
Nobody sits on this couch
This is the table where nobody eats
Nobody eats at this table
This is the bed that she sleeps alone in
She sleeps alone in this bed

Scattered sighs
Shattered dreams
Scattered thunder
So it seems

This is the mouth that nobody kisses
Nobody kisses this mouth
This is the body that nobody touches

Nobody touches this body
These are the breasts that nobody fondles
Nobody fondles these breasts
This is her belly that longs for a baby
The belly that longs for a child

Scattered sighs
Shattered dreams
Scattered thunder
So it seems

These are the days of winter and weeping
Winter and weeping the days
This is the clock that ticks through the silence
Ticks through the silence this clock
This is the cry that drowns in the pillows
Drowns in the pillows the cry
These are the tears that flow to the river
They flow to the river these tears

Scattered sighs
Shattered dreams
Scattered thunder
So it seems

Amanda Strydom

I have the good fortune of an aunt who travels the skies. Thank you, Bea, for this photograph, which could have been taken above the mountains of the kingdom of Vendale.

PROLOGUE

Vincent stepped through the tall, carved, wooden doors into his father's extravagant apartments. As a child, he had only ever been summoned to this place after doing something to warrant his father's disapproval. Vincent's eyes flicked to the band of carved panels, each one an intricate, artistic rendering of some past king and his glorious achievements. His shoulders slumped, and as on many occasions before, Vincent wondered what he could ever do to match up to his ancestors in his father's eyes.

Vincent squared his shoulders. *I am a man now,* he thought as an irritable furrow settled between his eyebrows. A movement called upon his attention. From the corner of his eye, Vincent's gaze met the sight of his rotund progenitor, standing with arms outstretched, while a tailor made adjustments to a fine crimson and gold brocade suit.

A pair of hard, brown eyes glanced up at him, but his father said nothing, and Vincent knew to be patient. He waited, hands behind his back, shoulders hunched and head bowed while the tailor finished his work. Even when the tailor packed shimmering fabrics away in a large suitcase, folding everything with tender care, the stern, older man with grey streaks highlighting his short, pitch-black hair, continued to admire the workmanship of the robe his valet slipped over his shoulders. Only after the tailor left did Vincent's father turn towards his son, a disapproving look twitching his greying eyebrows together. Vincent felt his father's piercing, judgemental stare at Vincent's less ostentatious outfit. He squirmed with his left foot, driving the tip of his boot into the soft carpet.

"So, you are determined on this hunting excursion of yours." His father stated, turning back to the full-length mirror behind him, a deep gully marring his brow.

Vincent nodded. "Yes, Father. The party leaves within the hour."

His father shook his head, turning back to his son. Vincent observed a look of incomprehension settle over the aging man's features. "I do not understand why you have chosen this waste of your time and energies, but you insist it must be done, and I have no reason to object outright." Vincent's muscles bunched above his nose and his hands balled into fists, but his father continued, unperturbed, "Just take your safety seriously. You know how your mother worries. You should honestly take her health into consideration."

"What will it take to please you, Father?" the resentment in Vincent's voice was unmistakable. "When I stay in the library, studying, you find I am too passive. When I walk in the park, I am too frivolous. When I go out hunting, I am wasting my time. What would please you? Is there anything I could do to keep you happy?"

A dismissive hand silenced Vincent's outburst. "Go. Do what pleases you. It is all you ever do anyway. Begone with you and see to your safe return."

Vincent turned on his heel with the first word of his father's dismissal. In his anger, he did not notice the wry tone of his father's voice, or the indication of concern that lingered in his deep brown eyes. Vincent marched out and paused. Tall doors swung closed behind him with a thud. He took a deep breath, but it did not calm him enough to relax his fists. His jaw clenching, Vincent strode along the carpeted hallway until reaching the main entrance.

Why does he always do that? Can he look at me? He never gives me any opportunity to explain anything. If he knew the real reason for this excursion, he'd never let me go, but why must I lie to him? He just assumes he knows everything. I wish he'd just listen, sometimes. This is all so infuriating!

Vincent still fought to compose himself by the time he stepped out through the main doors and down a series of low stairs, but his heart lifted ever so slightly at the sight of his friends who mounted up in response to his arrival. His page boy, held out the reins to him, and Vincent took them before stroking the soft muzzle of his grey stallion. The elegant creature lowered his head, and gently butted Vincent's shoulder. Unable to hold onto his anger longer, Vincent's lips twitched and a glint returned to his eyes.

As he grabbed onto the pommel of the saddle, a woman's voice called out from behind him, "Vincent, aren't you going to bid me farewell?"

Vincent returned his foot, which he'd raised to the stirrup, back to the ground with a sigh. He turned to face the slender woman in her fifties who approached him, her elaborate gown trailing a train behind her. She sailed over to him and pecked him on the cheek before adding, "Must you go so plainly dressed, dear? At least you should be clothed befitting your station if you're going to go through with this harebrained idea of a hunting trip."

His teeth bit down on his lower lip as he thought, *not her, too.* Out loud, he said, "Mother, I am dressed in well-tailored, finely woven garments fit for any nobleman. I have my trusty sword," he patted a decorated scabbard which hung from his right hip, "and good old Haldir." Vincent said the last with reverence as he stroked the neck of his patient steed.

Her voice rose, worry creasing the corners of her eyes, "But Vincent, is it safe? That brute is far from trustworthy!" The look she sent the horse had the creature pawing the ground and Vincent had to calm him with a gentle whisper and more stroking on the powerful neck. Then Vincent turned to face his mother, kissed her lightly on her cheek and swung into his saddle with a mighty effort, barely clearing the saddle in his agitation. The short sword hanging from his hip made coordination difficult and he cursed it silently, wondering whether it was even a good idea to take such a thing with him. He shoved it into the right position so it would not bother him further and his fingers ran over the familiar relief of a rampant stag on the hilt.

Scowling, he gathered the reins, and then his eyes fell on two young women who stood to one side of the open courtyard, one of them stifling a giggle behind her hand. He gazed upon her curvaceous form. Tendrils of her raven hair floated about her face in the caress from a light breeze. She lowered her hand and mouthed, "I believe in you."

Vincent nodded to his cousin and his lips twitched into a lopsided smile. Then he saw the disapproving look the other young woman sent him as she glanced from her friend back to him. Her face was serious, her stance regal, and Vincent felt the iciness of her gaze. He looked between the two once more, noting the difference. Madeleine, his cousin, encouraging and waving brightly; Catherine, disapproving, a reminder of everything he was not. *Catherine,* he thought. *Albert's intended. No, not any more. She has become*—he cut off the thought, whirling his horse and trotting over the cobblestones in a clatter of hooves, followed by the thunder of twenty more horses as his retinue went after him. Vincent did not spare a backward glance for his mother or the two young women with her. He looked ahead, thanking his luck for a beautiful azure sky and the freedom to do as he pleased for the coming weeks, irrespective of what his parents thought of the matter.

PART I

SCATTERED SIGHS

1

Gisela glanced over her shoulder. All was quiet around the wooden farmhouse, nestled amongst the foothills with the tall, grey peaks forming their ever-present backdrop. Gentle, summer sunlight streamed through a cloud bank, bathing the moss-covered shingles in golden light. A lamb bleated in the distance, and Gisela heard the snort of a horse from the paddock beside the barn. There were no people in sight. She scanned the homestead a second time, just to be certain and breathed a sigh of relief.

Becoming aware of her furtiveness, Gisela steeled herself. Her head whipped forward, a little furrow appearing above the bridge of her nose. She pulled a thick, knitted cardigan about her frame and strode into the lane. A hornbeam hedge shielded her from view, and Gisela allowed a second sigh to escape her lips. A mixture of excitement and guilt coursed through her, bringing indecision. She glanced down and her eye caught sight of the radiant, crimson skirt which flared in time to her step. It was then excitement won out.

She smiled as she turned her attention to the beauty of the afternoon; birds flitted about in the hedge and further afield, trilling their sweet melodies. The lazy buzz of insects droned through the air. Gisela took a deep breath, stretching her arms to encompass all she saw. Her pace slowed while she revelled in her freedom. Excitement at the prospect of her afternoon rushed through her. She suppressed the twinge of guilt by saying to herself, "This is what I want, more than anything. By the Almighty, no one should be allowed to smother my dreams."

Then, she clapped her hands as a giggle escaped her. Even her legs could not suppress her enthusiasm and Gisela skipped a few steps before composing herself again. She glanced down at the skirt once more. Bright, red cotton, finely woven—her finger brushed it with a gentle caress. *It's so beautiful*, she thought as she gazed upon the bands of white and blue ribbon and lace she had spent hours sewing onto the lower third of the garment. Gisela dragged her attention away from the skirt and glanced instead at the sun, gauging the time from its position. She bit her lower lip, setting off at a brisk trot, a satchel bouncing against her back with every step. Durable, brown leather boots thudded on the compacted surface of the lane.

Still running, Gisela came over a rise and a row of brick houses came into sight. She slowed to a walk once she crested the elevation, her chest rising and falling in rapid succession. She shook her head, allowing the two long, thick braids of coal-black hair to whip about her. Her purpose was firm now. There was no going back anyway. *My dream*, she thought. *I can do this. I must do this. The gods are with me. I cannot let it all go to waste. I will do this.* In response, Gisela's stomach clenched as her conscience surfaced the image of her stern father, his dark eyes flashing with disapproval. Gisela took another deep breath, banishing the thought and adding aloud, "He will be proud of me—in the end."

"Gisela!" a gruff voice called out from under one of the poplar trees which lined the road on the outskirts of the village.

Her head whipped up, eyes fixing on the owner of the voice, her heart pounding louder even than when she had been running. Deep in thought, she hadn't even noticed the man leaning against the tree trunk. Gisela swallowed hard. Her hands balled into fists as the man stepped forward, out of the shade.

He was short, with a broad-brimmed leather hat on his head. He raised his face to better see her, showing off the most prominent feature of his visage: his nose. It was impossible to look at anything else. The bulbous proboscis overshadowed thin lips and in conjunction with the brim of the hat, hid small, dark eyes from view. He wore thick leather garments and carried a double-barrelled rifle slung over his left shoulder.

"What are you doing away from the vineyards at this hour? Your father will be looking for you," he said, a glint of mischief in his obscured eyes.

"Oh, Hilarion! It's only you," Gisela exclaimed, elated, a smile lighting up her face. "What do you think?" she asked, twirling as she stepped forward, allowing the skirt to billow out. The crimson tint was eye-catching.

His face sincere, but laced with a hint of hunger, Hilarion said, "You look beautiful."

She laughed and turned towards the row of ochre houses, taking Hilarion by the hand and tugging him forward. Her exuberance was infectious, and he responded with a laugh of his own.

They walked in companionable silence for a bit, observing the activity in the street before Hilarion said, his tone serious, "Gisela, are you certain this is a good idea? I cannot begin to imagine what your father will have to say about this if he finds out."

"Please," she huffed, "can we forget about him for a moment. I'm here now, the 'damage', whatever that may be, is done. I just want to make the most of this one, most exciting day of my life. Can you give me that, at least? Nothing more is going to come of it. It's not like I'll get chosen anyway, I'm too old."

Hilarion nodded and shrugged when she turned her attention towards the village green where a large crowd gathered. People were jostling to get a better view of a small, raised stage which had been erected on one end of the field, nearest the town hall.

All thoughts of her father dissipated at the sight of the crowd and Gisela's heart skipped a beat when the onlookers took note of her and her skirt with the ribbon and lace trimmings. She stepped forward, and the crowd parted before her. She strode towards the raised, wooden platform, her head high, all other thoughts forgotten.

2

Hilarion watched the crowd part for Gisela, and then close in behind her. She was lost from view, and he considered pushing his way through the throng of people to better see the stage, but then his face lit up, stars shimmering in his eyes hidden beneath his hat. He turned and rushed towards a two-storey, brick building which stood at the edge of the green. A weather-stained sign hung above the doorway, and upon it was painted the image of a yellow hog with a green apple in its mouth. "The Golden Boar", the sign proclaimed in bold lettering.

Hilarion waved to the innkeeper's wife, a woman of middling age, her dark tresses wound up in a tight bun behind her head. She wore a bright white apron over her brown dress and stood watching the commotion on the green from the inn's doorway. She nodded towards Hilarion; then she motioned up and inward with her head. Hilarion smiled at her and nodded his thanks before rushing inside and up the stairway, taking two at a time. Hilarion came out into the sleeping hall and crossed over to the opposite wall where he leaned his rifle beside a window. Then he sat down on the window ledge, swinging his short legs over the side, so he was better able to watch the spectacle on the stage below. He grinned, his body lightening as he took a deep breath. He had found the best vantage point the village had to offer.

After a moment of gazing at the throng of people below him, Hilarion picked out Gisela on the stage. She had removed her thick, grey cardigan, and Hilarion gasped at the intricate embroidery the bodice of her dress revealed. He marvelled at the hours of work she must have put in to create the beautiful gown she wore. It reminded him of a time, many years before, when he had attended the annual harvest festival and met a young girl, so short she could not see the dancers performing the harvest dance. He found her weeping with frustration as she craned her neck, only to be jostled by some spectator who didn't see the little ten-year-old at their feet. Hilarion had crouched down and offered her a ride on his shoulders. Although he was short, it had given her enough height to view the performance she so ardently wished to see.

Now, as Hilarion looked down onto the scene before him. Eight young women stood ready on the stage, their different coloured skirts still—the calm before the storm. His gaze fell upon Gisela, whose red skirt drew the eye to her. Even at that distance, Hilarion sensed the radiance emanating from her. Her hair was loose, and her charcoal tresses reached below her waist. Hilarion's mouth gaped at her beauty. Was this really the little girl he held up on his shoulders eight years before? He could hardly fathom the change she'd undergone. He had, certainly, taken note of her transformation from little girl to young woman, but in that moment, as she stood poised, waiting for the music to begin, the changes struck home an arrow, straight to his heart. Gisela was beautiful, and he could not deny his love for her any longer.

Hilarion saw the accordion move in the player's hands before he heard the first strains of the music. In bemusement, he watched that split second where the musician was playing and the dancers started moving before the sound reached him. It added a sense of otherworldliness to the scene, and he revelled in Gisela's perfection. Her arms rose above her head in a smooth motion, fierce and powerful, then one arm gathered up her skirts and began the characteristic twirling of the fabric while her feet tapped out a series of steps. Everything about her dance drew Hilarion in deeper. He had eyes for her alone as she whirled and swung across the stage, her skirts billowing out from her waist, an undulating ocean of crimson fabric with its splashes of white and blue from the trimmings.

Hilarion forgot all else. Gisela's raw talent became

his whole world. Everything around her faded; the other dancers, the crowd of people. All paled into insignificance before the majesty of Gisela's dancing. He did not notice the other spectators holding their breath as he did, all eyes transfixed by the whirling red. He barely heard the music, notes of a familiar folk melody, which most would hum along with under normal circumstances; but on this day, one could have heard a pin drop. Everyone, the whole village and any bystanders from nearby farms come to support their family's dancer, all fell into Gisela's trance.

Then silence fell as the final notes of the melody dissipated. The motion of the dancers, too, stopped. Hilarion became aware of himself again. He took a breath, conscious for the first time in many minutes of this habitual act, and noticing he had held it in. *How long*? He thought. He shook his head as though waking from a dream. Every fibre in his body was tense. Hilarion leaned back, relaxing his arms and shoulders in a deliberate motion before swinging around again.

An urgency took hold of him. He heard the crowd break the silence, bursting into a jubilant cheer. Hilarion raced down the stairs, out the inn door and across the open space towards the stage. Arriving at the back of the delighted crowd, he began pushing his way forward. All civility forgotten, he shoved his way through, using his elbows wherever necessary. As he forced his way through the throng of spectators, he heard a woman announce, "Miss Gisela Winry wins the honour of representing the village of Ylvaton at the Annual Harvest Festival. She will dance as Harvest Queen."

Hilarion sucked in his breath. She had done it. She really had achieved her dream. He made it to the elevated, wooden platform just as the group of dancers separated; he saw several faces heavy with disappointment, but Gisela—Gisela was radiant. Her smile was a ray of sunshine bestowed upon the crowd as she curtseyed low three times. Then she turned to a woman who stood beside the accordion player. Her hair was milky-white, but notwithstanding her advanced age, she was wiry and strong.

Hilarion recognised Mrs Smith, the dancing instructor. According to rumour, Mrs Smith had been the best dancer the village had ever produced. Many of the older inhabitants recounted her beauty and talent, and Hilarion wondered whether Gisela's performance perhaps came close to that experience. He felt a growing understanding of what in previous years had only elicited a bemused shaking of his head. He observed old Mrs Smith taking Gisela by the shoulder as she spoke to the young woman. He saw Mrs Smith's broad smile, and when Gisela bobbed her head and turned away, back towards him, Hilarion saw an uncharacteristic radiance emanating from her large doe eyes.

When the winsome woman noticed him, Hilarion's heart skipped a beat at the glowing smile he received.

Embarrassed by the unexpected flood of emotion, Hilarion broke contact, sweeping the group of other dancers as he did so, and he noticed something. Gisela was by far the oldest participant in the audition. He knew she had turned eighteen a few weeks before, but he was struck by the other girls' adolescent faces. None of them could be older than sixteen. He saw awe in most of their eyes as they observed Gisela passing them. Hilarion noted a hint of jealousy in some of their faces.

Gisela's elegant, new dancing shoes rapped on the boards of the stage as she strode towards him, and Hilarion looked up again, beaming at her.

"You were amazing," he exclaimed, as she sat down at the edge of the stage and proceeded to unlace the dainty footwear.

She grinned at him, her hands still busy with her shoes, and winked. Then she returned her attention to her shoe, as though trying to suppress her pleasure at the compliment.

Unable to hold back his curiosity, Hilairon asked, "What did Mrs Smith say?"

She glowed, radiated warmth and energy at the memory. Her eyes closed, then sprung open again a second later as a smile spread over her face, igniting fires in her eyes. "She said," Gisela paused for effect, "that I'll be even greater than she was."

Gisela finished tying the laces on her heavy boots and slipped the dancing shoes back into the brown satchel. Then she slipped it over her arms and onto her back. As she hopped off the stage, Gisela glanced at Hilarion again, and added, "She wants to give me private lessons."

Hilarion paused, but Gisela walked off without looking back, thanking the bystanders who showered her with congratulations. Noticing he was falling behind, Hilarion set off after her, pushing past people once again. When they left the crowd behind, Hilarion saw Gisela make her way straight for the church, a small, white, wooden building set on the edge of the green. The elm-wood door stood open and she slipped inside. He chose to wait, not being fond of the place of worship which only reminded him of funerals.

3

Gisela crossed the dim nave of the church, passing between the pews and coming to stand before the stone altar. She breathed deeply, with precision, absorbing the cool, quiet of the place. Sunlight streamed through the windows behind the altar, casting gentle light on the massive stone block carved with undulating, scaled forms. Gisela closed her eyes, peace rising within her through the cold flagstones and enveloping her, softening every muscle in her body. She sank to her knees and whispered her gratitude.

"Thank you, oh great ones, for this opportunity. The possibility of dancing today has made me see clearly that this is what I want. I couldn't even see it before. I'm so grateful you find me worthy of such a great honour, and I'm humbled to have the opportunity to dance more. Thank you for this blessing." After a moment's silence, while Gisela fought with her thoughts, pushing down the desire to ask for more—to request guidance—she rose to her feet, her boots coming down hard on the stone floor. "This is bigger than me, but I must do it on my own," she muttered under her breath.

Determination blazed in her gaze when Gisela turned back the way she had come and stepped out into the warm afternoon sunshine. She saw Hilarion standing to one side of the door, his hat twisting in his hands. Gisela's face broke into a cheerful smile as she nodded in his direction before setting off through the village and back towards her home. As usual, Hilarion accompanied her, and she raised her eyes and thanked the heavens above for his friendship. He was very dependable, and she was grateful for it.

They walked in silence for a while, side by side, celebrating her triumph in their own way, before Hilarion sighed and said, "What are you going to tell your father?"

Gisela glanced over at her friend, but said nothing.

"Blimey, Gisela! You can't keep this secret from him. What are you going to do about your father?"

Her eyebrows pulled together. "You're no fun. Can't I think about that later? Training doesn't start until next week. I have a bit of time to convince him. I need to think about it a bit, but I'm sure he won't mind too much. After all, I am bringing the family honour by representing the village, aren't I?"

"You know that's not going to work for him," Hilarion retorted. "He's going to take one look at your skirt, and he's going to snap a thread. Blast it, Gise! You need a plan."

Gisela rubbed her forehead, then she threw her hand up in exasperation. "Can I have one evening to relish my triumph? I did it. I actually did it! Did you see me out there?"

"Yes, I did," Hilarion smiled in response to her exuberant gestures. However, he would not be deterred. "I saw you," he continued, "but your father did not. If I know anything of him, he'll be livid about the whole thing and he won't give you time to think about anything."

Gisela saw he wanted to keep talking, but she burst forth as her dark eyebrows drew together, "This stinks! Why do you always have to ruin everything?" She pushed him away from her, petulant. Then she turned away, crossing her arms and strode off, muttering to herself about how unfair the whole situation was.

Hilarion increased his pace, closing the distance between them, even though Gisela walked with brisk, purposeful strides. He grabbed her shoulder, whipping her around to face him, "I know it isn't fair," he said, and Gisela saw the tell-tale signs of anger smouldering in his eyes. "I know it's not fair," he reiterated, "but you have to see reason. If you march up there now and go into the house, he will see your skirt. Nothing ever passes him by. Don't you remember last year, at the festival, when all you wanted was to sneak off and watch the dancing? He found us, and I don't want to hear a repeat of the words he uttered then. I can only imagine it might even be worse."

Gisela watched as worry took over his expression. He held onto both her shoulders, an adult trying to make a child see reason. She bristled. Gisela felt her frustration crease her forehead even further. Her hands balled into fists. She tried to turn away, but Hilarion held her firmly. The turmoil of confused thoughts and emotions burst to the surface in an uncontrolled, haphazard feeling of rage. Gisela pushed him away from her, resolution burning within her. "Go home, Hilarion," she said with soft determination. "I'm not a child for you to coddle. I can manage my father on my own."

She glared at him before wheeling about and running for the remaining distance to her home. The lights in the windows glowed bright, and Gisela suddenly became aware of the time. The sun had set and only the last tendrils of light were being overpowered by the blanket of night. As she hopped over the gate in a smooth motion which indicated years of practise, Gisela noted the evening star which hung bright and clear above the high peaks in the distance.

"Mother of light," she whispered, "please let there be hope for me. Please let this work out... somehow. "

Gisela scurried towards the barn with every intention of hiding her crimson dancing skirt back where she had left her clothes earlier that afternoon, but as she slunk in the shadows, the front door to the farm house burst open with a loud crash, sending shuddering shock waves into the wall, which reverberated in the glass panes of the few windows. Light flooded the area between the house and the barn. Gisela was bathed in bright light and came to a standstill—frozen in terror.

"Where have you been?" Her father's indignation was unmistakable. "You were supposed to tend to the sheep, but—" he broke off. The tall, grey-haired man stood in the doorway, the light behind him throwing a long shadow over the footpath leading to the main house.

Gisela backed away at the sight of his eyes popping out of his head and his mouth hanging open. His shock at the sight of the red fabric disappeared in the blink of an eye. A muscle began to twitch in his jaw as he ground his teeth before unleashing a torrent of outrage. She crossed her arms, almost protectively over her body, holding her shoulders and crouching in on herself, as though lessening her size could reduce the impact of his outrage.

"You little skank!" he exclaimed, spittle flying. He lunged towards her, but came to an abrupt halt when strong arms wrapped about him from behind.

Through her terror, Gisela saw the vague outlines of her brothers, and she heard their strained breaths as they restrained their father. Tears rose unbidden, and

Gisela clenched her fist, allowing her fingernails to bite into her flesh. Her teeth came down on her lower lip. Then she whispered, "It wasn't supposed to be this way."

"No!" he screamed back at her. "You were supposed to do as you were told! You were supposed to be a good daughter, an honourable child, but you disgrace me —shame me."

One of her brothers grunted as her father continued to fight against their combined efforts. She wanted to stand up for herself, defend her actions, but as she began to speak, her eldest brother, Sven, groaned, "Give it a rest. There is no point arguing with him now." Then he called over his shoulder, "Mother!"

Gisela noted the desperation in his voice and she saw her father's elbow land a blow to his gut. She gasped as terror flooded through her. She became acutely aware her father was beyond reasoning. His fury had changed him. Her usually kind and gentle progenitor was a fiend, ready to strangle her where she stood. Her brothers tightened their hold, their youth and teamwork maintaining their firm hold on their father.

Then a voice emanated from the doorway. "Come, Gisela," her mother said.

Gisela assumed the disapproval she heard was aimed at her father, not at herself. Giving her father and brothers a wide berth, Gisela rejoined her mother on the threshold. "Up to your room," her mother said, bustling the teenager into the fire-lit communal room and towards rough-hewn wooden stairs. Gisela followed instructions and took them two at a time. The sound of her footsteps on the creaking wood diminished the sound of grunts and wheezes coming from the rest of her family.

Her mother followed her, and shoved her into the room, closing the door and bolting it behind them. "We'd better get your bed against here. There's no knowing what he'll do until he calms down, so we'd better not give him a chance to do anything he'll regret."

Together, they heaved and pushed the solid, wooden piece of furniture from one wall to the other, blocking the doorway. Gisela slumped onto the bed, unable to hold back the surging tears any longer. She buried her face in her hands and wept as the adrenaline, which had pumped through her before, released with the relief of safety.

A broad hand rubbed her back, and a soothing song brought back memories of her mother's comfort in days past. "There, there," the older woman whispered once Gisela's sobs subsided. "We'll work it out. Everything is going to be fine and your father will come to his senses."

With a sniff, Gisela pushed herself upright and wound her arms about the sturdy frame of her mother, resting her head against the bosom where she was reminded of the steady beat of her mother's solid, unconditional love. "Will he really?" she whispered, her voice breaking again as more tears spilled down her cheeks.

"Your father loves you, Gisela. Don't doubt that," her mother replied, and Gisela sat up again, wiping the damp trails from her cheeks. Firm arms tightened about her before dropping into the older woman's lap. "How did it go?" Curiosity lined her voice.

Gisela turned her large brown eyes onto her mother's, then dropped her gaze, as embarrassment and pleasure fought over the power for her facial muscles. "I'm Harvest Queen," she said.

Her mother gasped, a hand flying to her mouth, pride brimming in her eyes. "Oh, Gisela!" she exclaimed. "I knew you had it in you." They embraced again, and the older woman said into her daughter's hair, emotion tugging at her voice, "I'm so proud of you for doing this, for actually going ahead and reaching for your dream despite everything standing in your way." She pushed Gisela onto her feet again, as she said, "Let me take a good look at you."

She examined Gisela from head to toe, a smile lighting up her worn face. Then she brushed the skirt with her fingers, lifting the fabric. "You chose this well," she muttered as she flipped the fabric over onto her arm, exposing the back and the workmanship for the applications. Her smile grew even wider as she noted tiny, even stitching holding the ribbon and lace trimmings in place. "This," she said with satisfaction, "is very well done. Your mother taught you well."

A giggle bubbled inside Gisela, and her mother winked at her. They tumbled onto the bed, laughing and hugging. Calm filled the young woman resting in her mother's arms. She could not remember the last time she and her mother had spent time alone like this. Sometimes they'd be alone in the kitchen, but it had been years since they sat and talked. Warmth spread through Gisela, making her fingers tingle and bringing contentment with it.

Mrs Winry fetched a hairbrush from a wooden table that served as a dresser. She had to crouch low under the slanting roof, straightening with a hand to her lower back as a grimace crossed her once-smooth visage. She took an uneven step to return to Gisela who sat on the bed, twisting a strand of ebony between her fingers.

The brush pulled hair in a soft, rhythmic motion. Gisela half closed her eyes, basking in the attention and her mother's care. "I wish you had told me," her mother ventured at length. "I could have helped you with an alibi." Gisela remained silent, and her mother continued, "We were quite worried, not knowing where you were or what might have happened. Your father was beside himself. He thought something was afoot and was on the point of going out after you."

"I'm sorry," Gisela whispered. "I didn't think of the

part when I come home. I only thought about getting into town on time."

Dexterous fingers began the fast weaving that comes with many years of practise—left and over, right and over, left. Dark tresses smoothed into a thick braid. "You must have told someone," Gisela's mother continued, her tone unhurried.

She bit her lip but said nothing.

"Was it the gamekeeper's boy? Hilarion, right?"

Gisela stiffened, and her mother chuckled. "You think I haven't noticed him mooning after you?"

Gisela whipped around to face her mother, her eyes wide. "It's not like that. He's my friend!" Her mother raised a quizzical eyebrow and Gisela felt overpowering heat rush to her neck and ears. She dropped her gaze, insisting, "Hilarion is my friend, and yes, I did tell him."

Rough hands gently repositioned Gisela and took up the braid again, finishing off in silence and tying it with a ribbon. Then she switched sides and began with the second braid before murmuring, "You may believe him to be no more than a friend, Gise, but you must also be aware of what he wants. Does Hilarion, perhaps want something more?"

Gisela frowned, her voice indignant. "No!" Her mother kept braiding, so she added, "He would have said something by now, or..." she trailed off, hand rubbing her scrunched-up brow as though trying to efface a disgusting thought.

"What are the expectations for training in the role as Harvest Queen?" her mother asked, changing the subject while she tied the second braid and ran the brush over the end, smoothing the hairs in the tassel.

Gisela breathed a sigh, relief washing over her. Her muscles relaxed while she turned her attention to everything Mrs Smith had told her about training and launched into a series of explanations to her mother about how she would maintain her own duties at home as well as attend practise sessions in the village.

4

Hilarion watched until the gathering dusk swallowed Gisela in the distance. He rubbed his brow and turned to cut across a vineyard, heading towards the thick forest along the foothills of the mountain. He brushed a bright green leaf hanging from above as a heavy sigh escaped his lips.

"Go home!" her words echoed in his head. His arm slumped back against his side. It was unusually light. Something was missing. His left hand clutched at his shoulder, where a leather strap was wont to chafe his chest. Hilarion groaned, "Damn the evil and its minions!"

Hilarion set off at a trot, back the way he had come, still swearing under his breath as twinkling lights announced he was nearing the village. He stepped into the smoky, raucous inn and stepped up to the bar, his hat twisting in his hands. He cleared his throat.

"Ah, gamekeeper!" The woman behind the counter exclaimed. "Back so soon?" Her face creased into a knowing smile as she nodded towards his rifle, which leaned against the wall behind her. "Would you like to stay for a bite to eat tonight? Or did you catch that fish you were after earlier today?"

Hilarion's gut clenched at the tone in her voice and the look in her eye. A few of the other villagers snickered behind him, calling up a dark cloud over Hilarion's visage. Hilarion grunted. He grabbed the rifle she proffered, made an about turn, swung the mark of his office into place on his back and marched out the door without a backward glance. He ignored the loud guffaws that spilled out behind him as he strode into the dark.

They meant no harm, one part of him thought as he left the lights of the village behind him. *But they don't need to be so boorish either,* another replied. As the deeper darkness of the forest-covered foothills loomed nearer, he allowed the feeling of righteous anger to roll off him and turned his attention onto Gisela instead. Her contagious happiness after the audition lifted his spirits, which only came crashing down again as he wondered about how things were going for her at home. A shiver ran up his spine as he remembered her father's outburst, the autumn before, during the harvest festival. *Why does Farmer Winry despise dancers so vehemently?* Hilarion wondered as he pulled off his boots at the entrance to his humble shack.

It was fully dark, and the structure was overshadowed by the deeper obscurity of the tall trees standing around it. Hilarion trudged inside, hung his hat and gun on a crude-looking hook beside the door, and after a short while struck up a rush-light. He set about lighting the fire while he pondered Gisela's dilemma, but he could not focus on her plight long. His mind kept shifting to her glowing performance earlier that afternoon. Once a fire crackled beneath a heavy cast-iron pot, Hilarion sat back staring into the flickering light, reliving the flame in Gisela's gaze as she spun around, her skirts billowing out about her. Crimson flames. The warmth of her passionate smile. He wanted to reach out and brush her cheek, touch his lips to hers.

His grumbling stomach pulled him out of the daydream. Hilarion roused himself and ladled a congealing mass of overcooked vegetables dotted with the odd fatty lump into a wooden bowl. He proceeded to shovel the vittles down his throat with a wooden spoon. He sat cross-legged beside the fire, disregarding a stool and table that stood to one side of his one-room abode. The food disappeared into his mouth with automated precision. He did not savour it. It was sustenance, nothing more.

Once finished, he hopped up, strode out the door and rinsed the bowl, ladle and spoon in water from a half-full bucket standing beside the exterior wall. The water sloshed onto the hard ground beside the strategically placed flagstone where he stood. Excess fluid absorbed into a muddy patch. Once clean, he returned the items to a shelf on the wall. A cup and a few more spoons and a second bowl stood on the otherwise empty shelf.

Hilarion stepped outside once more, dipping his hands into the bucket to wash off the grime accumulated there. Then he splashed more water from the bucket onto his face. He shook himself, his hair fanning out around his head, and entered the hut. Hilarion pulled at the thong tied about his waist and peeled the leather casing from his body. An irritation grew between his shoulder blades and he scratched a few times.

He slipped into bed, a wooden structure resembling a rectangular box covered with a rough linen fabric. He settled in under the sheet, ignoring the prickle of straw raking his body through the undershirt and rested his head on an arm. He stared into the fire, which dimmed to glowing embers. His mind wandered back to Gisela and her father. Could he not do something to help her? He wanted to see her face glow like it had that afternoon. He wanted to be the cause for such happiness because it reminded him of a glow he'd once had, too, in days long passed. What could he do? How could he make her happy and grateful to him? Hilarion pondered his dilemma, drifting in and out of dreams. Her legs appearing when the skirts whirled up. The shapely turn of her thighs.

His mind travelled further in a half dream before drifting to sleep.

It was near dawn, when Hilarion sat bolt upright in bed. His nostrils flared, and a grin spread across his face. *Yes,* he thought. *That will most definitely work.* He swung out of bed and slipped back into his leather garments. Then, Hilarion set about his morning duties, clearing the hearth and saving the glowing embers that remained from the night before. He hummed a ditty as he went about his business, sweeping the dirt floor of his shack with deliberate care. Returning the besom to its place in a corner of the room, Hilarion stepped over to a large chest beside the bed. It was worn with age and use, and the hinges creaked when he lifted the lid. He rummaged inside, stopped to look at something with his head nodding a few times, as though counting something softly to himself. Then he nodded with greater emphasis, grunted as a half-smile played across his lips and shut the lid with practised care.

Soon after, Hilarion strode along a game trail under the thick canopy of trees. The green of early summer lit up as dawn approached. The air was clear, promising another bright, warm day, and it was aflutter with the chirping of euphoric birds. He whistled a tune and proceeded with a jaunty step. Seeing some hoof prints in a softer patch of earth, Hilarion bent down to study them, then smiled to himself before continuing on his way. He took his time, ambling along, stopping here or there to investigate a burrow or paw prints beside a stream. Contrary to the evening before, his mood was positively jovial, and it became increasingly buoyant as he proceeded on his way. Sunlight streamed through the trees, sending long fingers between gnarled trunks and showering the forest floor in luminescent green.

After about an hour of his haphazard journey, the trees began to thin, and Hilarion glimpsed the rising, verdant stalks of young wheat stretching out into the distance until they were halted by a row of cypresses, tall sentinels stretching out to brush the azure vault above them. He changed direction, following the border of the field, feeling his gaze being pulled along and upward by the snow-tipped crags rising beyond the thick woodland, which had obscured everything while he was in it. The sun's rays gleamed as they spilled over the majestic view, bathing all they touched in golden tones.

Hilarion paused, taking deep breaths. He absorbed the glory of life and listened to the cheerful trills of birds singing their joy of a new day. His eyes swept down the mountains, over a fenced-off paddock, which spread out where the wheat field ended, and felt his heart skip a beat as his gaze settled on a series of buildings. There was an ample farm house and a smaller barn, which stood at right angles to the main building. They welcomed him, or so he felt in the brightness of the summer sun and on the upbeat brought by this beautiful day. Hilarion set off again, quickening his pace as he approached the farmstead, craning his neck, straining to see if he could make out anyone in the courtyard.

Once closer, Hilarion saw a figure, dressed in simple brown, ambling from the main house to a well. It stood at the centre of the open yard, which was bordered on two sides by the house and barn, with a wooden rail fence closing off the other two extremities. The gentle sway of the person's hips, and the graceful way she moved, made Hilarion swallow hard even as his feet picked up speed in spite of himself. Gisela seemed different though. There was something about the posture of her shoulders and the way in which she dragged her feet ever so slightly. Hilarion's face twitched as he searched for a word. *Listless,* he thought after a moment.

He reached the fence and swung himself through the wooden posts, twisting his body to avoid his rifle from snagging on the wood. Gisela looked up at him when he hailed her. Hilarion bit his lip at the look she bestowed on him. Something about her was changed. He hurried to her side, a series of questions clamouring for supremacy, but Hilarion held them all back. He sensed it was not the time.

Gisela was already turning the crank on the well when he joined her. "I'll get that," he offered, extending a hand. She looked up, not meeting his gaze, and stepped aside so he could take over the strenuous work. Gisela said nothing. Hilarion chose to maintain the silence until she volunteered information. He was acutely aware something must have happened, but he knew Gisela well enough not to press her. It would be better to wait. He knew she would relent once she had found the words.

Hilarion lifted the heavy bucket off the well hook, and Gisela turned, heading towards the main house. He followed her a little unsteadily, as a splash of water sloshed to the ground. He bit down hard, his jaw muscle straining, but no more water fell. They entered the house and Hilarion deposited the full bucket where Gisela pointed. She glanced up at the dark recess beyond the stairs, and lifted an elegant finger to her lips. His heart constricted when he noticed the seriousness dominating her features.

She hurried out again and he followed, the sound of his boots heavy on the stone floor. *What ever has happened?* he wondered. She had never been this reticent, and he noted with apprehension she had not touched him once. Where was the gentle nudge, the friendly shove, or even a hug? Why would she not speak to him? With growing trepidation, Hilarion followed Gisela as she stalked past the barn and into the vineyard. She did not look back. With purposeful strides, she led the way through the rows of trellises to the far end of the cultivation. The sound of rushing water reached his ears and they approached the border hedge on the extreme end of the field. Gisela slipped through a narrow opening in the hedgerow and followed the bubbling brook beyond, until she came to a large boulder, which she promptly climbed.

Hilarion slipped his rifle off his back, leaned it against the hedge beside the rock and scrambled up beside her. She sat, dangling her legs above the stream and staring into the rushing water, as though she wished the laughing current could sweep her away with it. Hilarion looked about, absorbing the view of another wheat field with more vineyards beyond. Gisela maintained her silence, and Hilarion responded with an impatient grunt, a furrow forming above his large nose.

"Whatever happened?" he asked, unable to keep to his own council to wait for her to speak.

Gisela shifted, her fingers twined about the short tassel of hair at the end of a braid. She glanced at him, then looked away. She sighed. "Father did catch me right when I got back yesterday," she said at long last.

Hilarion felt his blood drain. A chill swept through him and he scrutinised her. He could not detect any bruises, and when he thought back on their walk to the rock, he could not remember her limping or showing any signs of damage. When he wanted to confirm his assumptions, Hilarion realised his voice had joined his drained blood, somewhere far removed from his mouth. His lips parted but no sound came out, so he shut them again.

He saw Gisela glance at him from the corner of her

eye. Then she sighed and continued, "Father cut up rough. I've never seen him so angry before. Sven and Robert had to hold him back." She closed her eyes.

Hilarion observed her facial muscles contorting with pain. He wanted to comfort her, to tell her he had found a solution, but his voice remained lost in the depths of his being, unattainable.

"Mother and I spent the night locked in my room, and this morning, I was woken when Sven told us they were going into town with Father to speak with Mrs Smith." Her voice cracked when she added, "I think he wants to convince her to revoke her decision." She lifted her hands, burying her face in them and stifling a sob.

His instinctive move was to place a comforting hand on her shoulder, and as he did so, the lock which had held back his voice clicked open and the flood-gates swung wide. "Gisela, this is unnecessary and unfair," he began, trying to control the tremor in his voice. "You should not have to suffer this way. I want you to be happy, as you were when you were dancing on that stage yesterday. More than anything in this world, I want you to be able to do what you love."

She shifted her torso, facing him, her hands resting in her lap while her large chocolate eyes turned on him in wonder. "How?" she ventured.

Excitement sweeping him away, Hilarion grabbed her hand and said, "Marry me. I will be a good husband to you, and I will let you dance all you want.

You could be Mrs Smith's replacement and train the new dancers every year. Perhaps we could travel—" He broke off. A blank look crept over her face. *She is in shock*, he realised, and in the next instant, he saw a mixture of revulsion and anger flash at him. She grabbed back her hand, sprung to her feet and rounded on him.

"How would that help?" she shouted. "The Harvest Queen is a pure, unmarried woman. I would be dropped from the festival instantly. And can you imagine what my father would say?"

She paused a moment, then straightened as she continued, "The rumours with a hasty wedding will have my father either kill you, or me—or both of us. Have you gone spare?" Gisela spat the last before whirling about, leaping from the rock and running back the way they had come. Hilarion was stunned. He sat, immovable at first. Then, he pulled his knees up, crossed his arms over them and rested his head as he berated himself, *Stupid, stupid, stupid.*

5

Fury lent Gisela strength. She traversed the vineyard, her head high, the image of Hilarion's simpering expression sending a shudder through her. Gisela raged. *What a prat. How could he even think that was a solution?*

She grazed her hand against the rough fabric of her skirt. It stung, but she embraced the discomfort of a layer of skin abrading from her hand as though rubbing the skin off might remove the memory of Hilarion's unsolicited touch. Another shudder coursed through her as she tried to block from her memory the way he leaned towards her, looking at her with expectant delight from under his hat.

How could he think I would do such a thing? A marriage for convenience.

Her mind made the next leap, to a life living with

him, eking out an existence in his tiny shack with its dusty floor. The poverty he lived in had always bothered her, but now, at the prospect of living that way herself, she rejected it even more firmly. *What kind of place would that be for raising children?* Children... her mind lurched to the next thought. The memory of his hand on hers, sticky with sweat. Those hands on her body. She convulsed again, scraping her hand on her skirt once more. *No, no, no*, she raged in her mind. *This is not what I want. This is not how life should be.*

A sudden thought stabbed through her mind. It was a lightning strike that stopped her in her tracks. The anger vanished in a puff. It was replaced with another feeling. Visceral. Unnerving. She struggled to place it. Her breath caught in her chest. It was the response to the look of hope in his eyes, the knowledge he was trying to help her no matter how loathsome the outcome was to her. *He cares about me, and my reaction was heartless.* How could she have rejected her friend in such a cruel and inconsiderate manner? *He will never forgive me for it*, she thought as tears mounted, sending a constricting lump to her throat.

Gisela registered with horror the final look of shocked hurt he had given her for her outburst. Knowing she had hurt his feelings sent raw pain raking through her heart. He was her friend. She had not intended his kindness and friendship to end in this way. *Harsh! Unfeeling!* Her hands raised to cover her eyes, blocking out the sunny day, bringing darkness to match what she felt within. *What have I done?* Again, the memory of his gaze swam into her vision, unrelenting reminder of how irreversible this was. Her reaction—no, overreaction—was taking the trust of friendship from her. Hilarion had been her friend, and she trusted him. She shared everything with him. *Could there be a way to overcome this lack of attraction she felt? To accept his offer?*

Gisela shook her head. *No,* the conviction was commanding, unwavering. *I do not love him like that.* Friendship, though, that was special. It was sacred, and she had thrown it away with her spontaneous, inconsiderate reaction. She stared up into the blue and a shriek burst from her. Loss. It was so great it pulled her downwards as the sound rose up. Her knees knocked onto the hard, dry ground. She barely felt the contact. Nothing physical could tear her from the ravages of hindsight. *Why?* The thought pounded through her brain.

"Why?" Gisela screamed up into the cloudless sky, the beauty of the day mocking the agony she felt within. If only the sky could be pelting rain, to wash away the guilt which wrapped itself around her heart and squeezed, constricting everything in a haze of emotional pain more powerful than she ever believed possible. *Friendship—betrayed. Trust—broken. Love—cruelly rejected.* "Why?" she raged again, but in a strangled sob.

Because I don't love him, the answer came back. It

was undeniable. His eyes, resurfaced again, taunting her along with her mother's words. *You think I haven't noticed him mooning after you? You may believe him to be no more than a friend, Gisela, but you must also be aware of what he wants.* Helplessness overwhelmed her. There was no comfort out in the streaming sun as it beat down on the vineyard. Her whirlwind thoughts pelted her and opened the floodgates. Launching to her feet, Gisela ran. Tears streamed and her nose burned. She did not stop until she reached the safety of her home where she flung herself on the floor, giving full sway to the emotional torrent coursing through her.

When she came to her senses, Gisela heard the gentle timbre of her mother's voice crooning at her in her habitual soothing manner, but it only made Gisela feel worse. She had been callous of her friend's feelings even though her mother had warned her it might be so. *What have I done?* She repeated to herself, bringing on a renewed bout of sobbing. Gisela lost all sense of time. Emotional exhaustion tugged at her as she drifted between bouts of self-recrimination and more tears. Her mother never left her side, but Gisela was unable and unwilling to share the cause of her distress. She did not hear her mother's soft song, a memory from her childhood. She was oblivious to the return of her brothers, calling joyfully—then stopping on the threshold, worry filling their voices. She was deaf to her father's constricted query and her mother's helpless shrug.

Deep in the depths of her own darkness, Gisela did not feel strong arms lifting her. She did not notice being carried up the stairs and slipped under the soft, white sheets. Eyes wide, she stared, unseeing. Her world filled with despair at her self-inflicted loss. At long last, she gave way to the gloom, drifting into unconsciousness brought on by fatigue.

Gisela came to her senses in her room. The half-light in the small, windowless space matched the heavy shadow inside her. She felt empty. Sleep had brought no reprieve. A dark, gaping hole with raw, jagged edges had settled in her chest cavity. Her mind was blank. Thick, glutinous mud coagulated in her brain, making it impossible to think. She lay in bed a long time until the sounds reaching her ears found their way into her mind. Soft muttering, laced with worry, reached some deep recess of her self and propelled Gisela to action. It took an extraordinary effort to sit, but at long last, she managed to push herself into the upright position. From there, her muscles took over in mechanical fashion, remembering the motion even if the intent was clouded.

She came down the stairs. Her mother and eldest brother stood by the sink washing and drying dishes. Her father sat on his customary stool by the kitchen table, and her other brother strode across the space towards the doorway, saying, "I'll go and check on the sheep."

On the final step, the wood creaked beneath her weight, and all eyes in the room snapped onto her. Wanting to be with her family but without actually being the centre of attention, Gisela avoided looking at any of them. Her brother stopped in his tracks, suspended in mid-stride, his words cut off as he looked up at her. The silence dragged on while Gisela, uncaring, drifted to her habitual place at the table. She sat without a word. The concerned glances shared between her family came to her as though from a great distance.

After a moment, sitting quite still, Gisela's mind latched onto the scarred surface of the mahogany kitchen table. A crack close to her caught her eye, and while her mind wandered to distant paths concerning the history of said table, her finger traced the scar in the wood. *How old is it?* she thought. The table was a sturdy, unchanging part of the kitchen. She could not remember a time when it had not stood there in the middle of the kitchen. *Was it already here when Grandpa Sven built the house?* she mused.

At some point, the hushed whispers of encouragement and meaningful looks passing between her mother and father did register in her conscious mind. When her father cleared his throat, Gisela heard it and turned her gaze upon her progenitor, but her motions were lethargic. At long last, she met her father's gaze and waited for him to speak. He cleared his throat a second time before affirming, "Gisela. After deliberating with Mrs Smith earlier today, I have come to the conclusion that representing our family and village at the regional harvest festival will be acceptable."

Silence. Gisela stared at her father, her brain a swirl of grey clouds. "What?" she asked, a quizzical frown raising her eyebrows.

"You may dance," he rephrased. "Under one condition."

Gisela struggled against the leaden nature of her thoughts. Why was everything going so slowly? She grasped the meaning of the words, but still, the lightness she knew was there held back, weighed down by her exchange with Hilarion.

One condition, she reiterated in her mind. "And what is that?" she asked, her voice still depressed. She did feel a gleam beginning to light her up again, though.

Her father breathed deeply, closing his eyes for a moment as relief coursed through him. "You shall give thanks in the church every day you go into town for rehearsals."

On any other day, Gisela would have laughed. The thought he had to give her such a task—when she did it willingly anyway—was almost absurd, but mirth had been ripped out of her. The weight of her loss, her undone friendship, was a pair of sandbags holding her soul tethered to the ground. All she could do was nod, and her father accepted it.

Her mother wiped damp hands on a kitchen towel and crossed over to where Gisela sat. She responded to her mother's embrace by leaning the back of her head against her mother's chest. The door thudded closed behind Robert, off to check on the sheep. At last, Gisela noticed the worried look passing between her parents, and she made an effort, sitting up and giving each a drawn smile.

"I'll be all right," she said. "I'm just knackered."

"Are you hungry?" her mother asked. Gisela shook her head to which the older woman replied, "Then get some sleep, luv. I'll leave something out in case you get hungry later."

Gisela nodded. She rose to her feet, the bench scraping against the rough flagstone floor. When she was in her room again, she turned her mind back to Hilarion. The perturbation wasn't as raw any longer. It was as though she looked at the situation from a great distance, dampened by the emptiness left from her emotional disintegration. Gisela sat a long time, perched on the edge of the mattress, her hands clasped in her lap. She sank onto the pillow at length and thought, as sleep cloaked her in serenity accompanying acceptance, *I can't marry him, because I can't make him happy—and, by the gods, that would be unfair. I don't love him and he is so deserving of a true, deep and meaningful love. It would be unfair and cruel of me to leave him in a loveless marriage. I can't do that to him.* She shuddered in that place of truth between waking and sleeping. *No. I respect him, and that's why I had to reject him. Although that, too, was cruel. I only hope, one day, he'll be able to forgive me.*

6

Hilarion sat on the rock, deaf to the sweet bird-song; blind to the vista stretching out before him. His thoughts turned inwards to his heart, which had been plucked out and thrown to the wild creatures of the forest. A single tear rolled down his cheek as he relived the acid in Gisela's tone and the rejection flashing in her eyes. Her reaction plunged him into a place he had been before. He knew this fuzzy grey spot well—the location where all thought became heavy and oozed instead of flowing as it should. Trained preservation took over. *Walk*, he ordered himself.

With leaden legs, Hilarion came to his feet and clambered down the rock. His hand went out in an automatic motion, swinging his rifle onto his back. The familiar, cool touch of the metal barrel was a soothing balm to reduce his agony-induced stupor. All power of thought lost, Hilarion's feet took over, taking him upstream until he reached the forest and then along winding game trails, moving ever onward. One foot in front of the other. The deliberate motion of walking, left then right, then left, then right again, settled the misty fog in his skull. Once it lifted, however, he could not keep the thoughts and memories at bay. They swirled and tormented him, driving him forward in the hope his feet might find the path out of the forest in his mind.

He had gone about it all wrong—started at the wrong end of the story. He should have begun with his plans, his dreams—the ones that matched hers. Instead he had botched the whole thing and driven her away. *What will come of it all now?* he wondered. His mind lingered on the pouch of coins hidden in his clothes-chest. Years spent saving, frugal meals, reducing all his expenses—and for what? It was all for nought because he had gotten ahead of himself and messed it all up.

Gisela's smile came next. For so many years, he had lived to receive her silent joy: outpouring sunlight to warm his withered heart, and now he was left with nothing. The barren darkness of his loneliness stretched ahead of him like a curse. *Yes, cursed*, he thought. *I always knew it was so. Why should Fate have changed anything when she made it clear years ago I belong to her and her alone.* Fate. Life. They were cruel mistresses, and no one knew that better than Hilarion.

His feet crossed a stream, stepping from one stone to another, crossing without any water reaching his boots, but it was a heavy sure-footedness—stoic and unwavering. All the while, his mind spiralled down, shearing off layer upon layer of a light cloak he had woven over the course of eight years—ever since a pair of tearful brown eyes had looked up at him in ecstatic joy when he offered to lift a young girl to watch the dancers at the harvest festival. The golden light he had comforted himself with had to go. All of it. *She is a selfish, superficial cow, and she deserves the fate in store for her. She deserves to suffer.*

Deep in some unknown recess of his self, some inky blackness shifted. It remained unnoticed by his conscious self, but his subconscious did register the sinister stain. It was the seed of a creature growing out of Hilarion's disdain for himself and his disbelief in his own worthiness. Ever since his family had been taken from him, he had believed with a fervent, unwavering belief that he was not meant to be happy—unworthy. Now, those thoughts reaffirmed by Gisela's actions, something ugly began to spawn, but he was too preoccupied to really notice.

Hilarion's brows were drawn together in a horizontal line, cleaving his forehead with his anger and disappointment. "Let her father have her. They deserve each other," he muttered. His grim self-righteousness pushed aside the small voice which jumped to her defence. No, he would not hear of it anymore. His life was darkness. He had seen the disgust in her expression. She could not bring herself to love him because he was not beautiful as she was. Her superficial nature, wanting pretty trappings and baubles, demanded another, more fitting partner. What was love? "Hah!" he spat. *Love.*

The emotion joined Gisela's defender, relegated to his subconscious. Hilarion had no need of such things. He was hard. Befriended by the cold and dark. He was the diamond that had been cut by life, and he knew his moment would come. He could take the money he had saved and leave. Go far away and start a new life. Perhaps he might even find a more pragmatic woman who would accept a decent offer when she received one. Hilarion breathed in deep breaths, pushing against the constricting bands that threatened to squeeze the life out of his chest. Loneliness was not a problem. He had conquered it before. *I can do it again.* His eyes flashed, and his jaw set with determination. "I can do it again," he reiterated.

Another breath. Air flowed through his nose, sweet and clear into his lungs which were finally able to absorb it again. Hilarion sensed the blood rushing. *I am full of life*, he thought. Ah life. "Cruel, twisted fate. Take everything from me and still leave me to live. What life do I have?" He smiled. It was a grim, mean smile, as though he shared a dark joke with his makers. Bitter and yet funny.

The next breath brought him to the tips of his toes,

his fingers outstretched, raking the green canopy and the celestial blue beyond as though he wished he could expose the blackness he knew lurked behind those bright colours. The beautiful things were just the trappings, lulling a person into a sense of security. Then fate got bored and everything turned to the ashes they actually were. *Curse her. Curse her and her stupid father.* His gaze returned to the path he followed, his mind once again aware of where his feet were taking him. *She deserves all the suffering that man causes her. I am better off without her.*

His face hardened at the bitterness of his thoughts. Yes, he wished never to lay eyes on her again. "Perhaps it is a good idea to move on," he mused. "The King's Forest is big. There will be other parts where a gamekeeper can make a home."

Hilarion hitched up the rifle, which had slipped. He stroked the leather strap crossing his chest. It was his steadfast mooring point, the one thing to always bring his mind out of the darkness and back to life, no matter how grim it seemed. He was high in the mountains, almost at the edge of the tree-line where the highland pastures began. Hilarion turned his feet up the gradient. Soon he came out above the trees onto a sunny glade where sheep tore at the lush grass in rhythmic munches. He climbed onto a boulder and looked out over the valley below. The sunlight sparkled off the serpentine loops of the river, far in the distance. Perfect rows of plantations stretched over most of the open plains between the forest and the dotted houses of the village.

He could just make out the white spire of the church. Gisela's sanctuary. The place of death he did not enter because it reminded him of his parents. The last time he had set foot in a church, he had worn black—some borrowed suit with the sleeves and legs folded up and stitched so the added length didn't show too obviously. *Loneliness.* The memory of Gisela dancing swam into his mind's eye; her face turned upward, thanking the sky for the rapture and glory she felt in every movement. Each motion was a natural expression of perfection, her whole being a blessing to those who observed her.

"Ha!" he shouted his defiance at the clouds.

Hilarion's gaze swept the vista again. He was king of the world, he could overcome a little rejection. He was master of all before him. Master? Not quite. For he knew, deep down, in the well of his shattered soul, that no matter how disgraced he felt, he would return to Gisela time and time again. He was the moth and she the flame. It was irrelevant that he knew better. It was obvious as he pondered her dancing and his heart rate increased with the memory of her whirling form. He would go back and watch her dance over and over again, no matter how often it burned him.

7

Vincent stifled a whimper as he hauled himself into the saddle. A week of riding had brought his body no closer to tolerating the punishment. Everything ached. With tender care, he squeezed thighs and calves to the rounded back and belly beneath. Then the rocking motion began, chafing the sore muscles in his buttocks. He groaned softly and wondered why, exactly, he had set off on this journey in the first place.

The face of his cousin, Madeleine, surfaced in his mind as she whispered, "I believe in you." She had said it right before his departure. Yes, this was all her fault. He rubbed the hollow in his lower back, trying to soothe the aching muscles while he thought of Madeleine's pixie face smiling up at him, goading him with sparkling eyes and her incessant questions. What of the people? Did he not wish to know how they lived?

What about the country? Seeing places. Her voice drifted into his mind, "I know you're in a bind, Vincent. Take this time to think, to live, to experience the world so you can tell me all about it when you get back. At least you can go using this pretence. Live for both of us, even if it's just for a little while."

It wasn't only Madeleine's constant pushing which convinced him to leave. Vincent needed to get away for other reasons. This so-called hunting expedition was the perfect opportunity to distance himself from his mother's wringing hands and the worried half-moons that creased her forehead whenever she looked at him. It also gave him space from his father with the disappointed gaze and heavy sighs. Then his mind took an about-turn and brought another face into view: chocolate eyes so sharp, they never missed anything; thin lips often pulled into a disapproving pout. Catherine. Her whole demeanour sent all his courage scurrying for cover in the inner depths of his rib cage.

Vincent couldn't help but remember the last look she gave him as he left. Catherine's sour glare, which had passed from him to Madeleine in that last minute as his horse wheeled about. The memory of her face brought an icy chill to the pit of his stomach. He rubbed a hand over his brow, trying to efface the recollection. His intestines knotted further, despite all attempts to remain calm. *I needed to get away. Thankfully, the ruse of a hunting trip threw them off the scent.* He knew his father would never have allowed him to leave if he'd admitted his real purpose. His mother would also have tailspun into a state of panic knowing he wanted to spend time among the common folk. *No, it is better they think I'm off on a four-week bender, hunting and carousing with my men somewhere in the King's Forest. My true interests have always been a source of anxiety and disdain. Nothing good could have come of telling them the truth.*

Kicking his grey mount into a trot, Vincent hurried forward to the head of the column. He pulled up beside the buff frame of his best friend, Oskar. A roguish smile met Vincent's gaze, lightening his mood.

"You mentioned we'd reach Port Averly today."

"Yes, old sport. It's quite a sight. Just wait until your eyes meet the deep blue. You'll never be the same again, I promise. And the women... ah, the women of Averly are the best in the whole kingdom. No one to rival them, except perhaps those exotic creatures from across the sea. We could journey to Erdalbad to see if the rumours are true. Now *that* could be quite the adventure, wouldn't you say? Something to regale our friends with, back in Realtown."

Vincent snorted and rubbed a hand over his clean-shaven jaw. "Father would have my head, not to mention your liver for dinner." He grinned and glanced over, catching sight of Oskar's crestfallen expression.

"You're such a spoil-sport, Vince."

"I am too important to have fun, remember. This

trip is it. Four weeks and nothing more. So, we'd better make the most of it before we're expected to take on our responsibilities."

A shudder ran through Oskar's tall frame. "Vince, please," he grumbled. "Don't mention the "r"-word again on this expedition. It makes me seedy. I just want to escape from it all."

Vincent nodded, his thoughts turning inward again. Escape; now that sounded just right. But for how long? He was back under Catherine's piercing gaze. He could sense her foot tapping under her floor-length skirts, as it so often did. Impatience, disapproval and control were her defining characteristics. *Why her*? he mused. *Why do they insist it has to be Catherine?* Out loud he said, "Yes, no need to let the crows loose. We've escaped that cage for a while. Let's not think about any of it."

"Jolly good," his friend conceded.

Vincent glanced about him. The valley had opened, spreading out into soft, low-lying hills which glinted golden in the sunlight. *Wheat*, he thought. *The breadbasket of Vendale—quite the fitting title.* His mount topped a rise and his eye caught sight of the sheer azure expanse which twinkled in the distance. Not far away, he saw the sprawling rooftops of the harbour town.

With a deep breath, Vincent banished all thoughts of Catherine and his parents. *I am here to learn anything and everything I can. I am free to experience what I wish, how I wish. This is the purpose of my journey.* Vincent squared his shoulders, resettling himself in the saddle, and smiled as Oskar let out an exuberant whoop, kicking his steed into a fast trot. "Last one to Averly is a nincompoop!" he shouted over his shoulder.

Laughing outright, Vincent squeezed with his legs, the aches of his body forgotten in his moment of abandon.

Two hours later, Vincent emerged from the "Lion's Inn" dressed in a simple cotton shirt and workman's trousers. He gave a furtive glance around him as he stepped onto the cobbled street while Oskar, clothed in similar peasant garb, swaggered out with his hands pressed deep into his pockets and his chest puffed out.

"Stop strutting around like a peacock," Vincent admonished, stepping up beside his friend. "You're drawing attention. The whole purpose of being in disguise is to go unnoticed."

"Oh, Vince," Oskar exclaimed. "You do like to ruin my fun! Besides, mingling with the commoners is your purpose, is it not?" Vincent nodded, his attention on the bustling docks at the end of the street. "Then where is the problem? I'm garnering precisely the right kind of attention."

Vincent noted Oskar winking meaningfully at a

group of young women beside a fountain a little way ahead of them. Giggles erupted in reply.

"You are incurable, my friend," Vincent said, shaking his head. "I am far more interested in the dockworkers and the market." Oskar's shoulders sagged and Vincent noticed the sigh that crossed his friend's lips as he turned his attention away from the group of curvaceous women. Oskar and Vincent sauntered off, followed by a burst of outright laughter.

The salty tang on the sea breeze was the first thing to hit Vincent. Next, he was drawn into the commotion of the docks teaming with men scurrying this way and that, carrying crates, their biceps bulging. He allowed the intense noise of men shouting instructions to each other to wash over him. The sounds of human activities were also joined by the constant swish of the waves lapping against the harbour wall in a never-ending whisper. Wooden ships creaked against the swell of the water, wind whistling through the rigging. Winches groaned under the load of heavy crates.

Vincent's legs froze with the weight of sights and sounds bombarding him. His senses were overwhelmed by the whole experience. He hardly knew which sound to respond to. He turned his head in every direction in short succession, following the strange sounds he could not place. Someone bumped into him from behind and Vincent's stammered apology was met with a stream of curses. Watching the still grumbling sailor totter off, his arms straining against the weight of his load, Vincent wondered how anyone could navigate this chaos.

As he inched away from the teeming quay, Vincent realised Oskar was nowhere in sight. An icy lump formed in the pit of his stomach. *Where is he?* Vincent thought. He glanced about him in mounting panic. He spun around again, frantic. *What can I do?* he asked himself. The terror of being lost for the first time in his life muddied his thoughts, and Vincent cast about himself blankly, unable to respond to his situation.

Then, his gaze picked out a familiar face. Across the street, beneath the overhang of a warehouse roof, stood a robust man. His angular face with a pitch-black moustache above the lip sent a wave of relief washing through Vincent. The man nodded to him and Vincent smiled. *Nothing to worry about*, he thought. *I'm not lost after all.* He gazed out to sea once more, observing the majestic ships swaying on the gentle swell. Their sails were furled and seagulls cried as they wheeled above the forest of masts.

Vincent watched a line of seamen snaking their way from the dock to a warehouse a short distance away. The yellow-brick building squatted low and vast. Brown bricks identified it as belonging to "Lindon and Co." Vincent stared at the warehouse and watched the men going in, carrying wares, and others coming out, arms swinging at their sides.

A thought sparked into Vincent's consciousness. Before he'd even formulated anything concrete, he stepped into the crowd, which sucked him into the flow, buffeting him about before spitting him out a few paces from the green gate to Lindon's warehouse.

Vincent peeked inside the dim building filled with towers of stacked crates and barrels. At the far end, light streamed through a doorway and Vincent heard men's voices undulating in the tone of conversation. *What am I doing here? I have no need for work.* Then Madeleine's voice popped into his mind: "Be open to new experiences," she had said. *I have not worked a day in my life,* his thoughts responded. *Perhaps today is as good as any to gain that experience.*

8

Gisela soared. The music lent her wings and set her free. Her feet navigated the steps with practised precision and such lightness, she barely felt the wooden floorboards of the city hall beneath them. The whirling of her skirts, each motion of her hands, the dynamics of the whole came so naturally to her, she allowed her thoughts to float. Flight: escaping and soaring—at the same time.

She embraced her liberty, rising into the azure skies of a magical realm bathed in golden sunlight, far removed from dark heartache and daily drudgery. The tones surged upward, taking her soul with them into a realm of peace and harmony, where all is calm. *I love this place,* she thought. *I could stay here forever, just floating.* Her eyes closed, Gisela allowed the notes of the accordion to shower her with joy, to fill her emptiness until she brimmed with life, serenity and elation. The overflowing emotions poured into every movement, adding vibrancy to the lightness she felt. Higher and higher she soared, ecstasy in the freedom of motion.

Then the music stopped. Stillness enveloped her, and Gisela was dragged back into the reality of her body, heaving for air in the aftermath of her exertion. Wings ripped from her soul, it came crashing back to the ground. Her eyes opened to the crowd which gathered to watch her every practise day, and fell upon that haunting, familiar face. Hilarion looked up at her. His demeanour was stern and the grimness in his eyes drove her spirit even lower. It sent her heart back into the black pit she had left behind while dancing. Every day she danced, he stood there and watched her, and then, before she could approach him, he vanished. Each time she hoped he might allow her the opportunity to explain, and always, he disappeared before she could reach him through the crowd of congratulating onlookers.

Gisela met his gaze and implored him with her eyes. *Please wait,* she pleaded in her mind. *Please let me talk to you!* With a sinking heart, she watched him stiffen. Then he spun about and marched out the hall into the pouring rain outside. *Hilarion!* she cried in the silence of her mind, closing her eyes again, plunging into a world of darkness equal to what she felt.

Brushing her hands over her face, wiping away the hurt she felt, Gisela turned and walked over to her bag, pulling off her dancing shoes in a numb motion. Her eyebrow twitched in frustration. *He has every right to make me pay for how I treated him*, she sighed. Swallowing hard to banish the tears threatening to well up, Gisela shoved her shoes into the satchel and pushed her feet into her worn boots. As she tied the laces, she yearned for the lightness that came to her with music. Gisela turned to leave and caught the eye of Mrs Smith. The wizened woman's nut-brown face beamed up at her. An encouraging nod brought an automatic smile to Gisela's lips.

Her instructor's support and the dancing were what kept Gisela going. As the days dragged on into weeks, Gisela fought the numbness within. She missed Hilarion's company. She missed spending every free moment with him. He had been a sturdy rock in the emotional turmoil of her life, and his friendship had meant much to her. Since their altercation at the beginning of the summer, she had not confided in anyone. Not talking was a burden on Gisela, for she was used to being a chatterbox. *I have no one, though*, she thought. Her brothers wouldn't understand. They were so focused on helping their father in the vineyard, and she had never been particularly close to her mother.

Her dancing companions scared her, too, for Gisela saw the envy in their eyes as they appraised her before and after the practise sessions. Most of them were rebuked during their performances, but never Gisela. Mrs Smith only ever showered her with praise, and

Gisela began to feel the sting of being the teacher's favourite. Being singled out did not help her in the least, and she knew she could not trust any of the other girls, even more so because she was the eldest in the group. She smiled at Katja, who straightened at the same time Gisela rose to her feet, but the sixteen-year-old's glare shrivelled Gisela's attempt at friendliness. As always, Gisela slunk out of the hall on her own, shoulders sagging in response to the weight the world had placed there.

She ran the short distance to the church, sloshing through the water-logged grass on the green. Gisela embraced the cold drops as they beat down on her exposed arms and face. Physical discomfort was a welcome relief from all the worries. After wringing out her hair, Gisela stepped inside the sanctuary and allowed the wave of despair to pour from her. Twice a week she danced in the village green (weather allowing), and twice a week she sought solace in the abandoned quiet of this place of worship.

Through sobs, Gisela asked, "Why does it all have to be so hard? Why does everyone who could be my friend shun me so? Why do I have to be alone?" The ungratefulness of her own words ringing in her ears, Gisela bit back her tirade and added, "I'm grateful. I truly am. I could not survive any of this without the dancing. I love to dance so much. Thank you, Mother-dragon, for the ability to dance."

She brushed a hand over her cheek, rubbing away

the sticky trail of tears that clung to her skin. "I want to do better," she said, taking a deep, deliberate breath. "I want this loneliness to end."

Looking up into the chiselled kindness of the effigy above her, Gisela continued, "Please help me. I need some sign that this will end, that I have paid my penance. Have I not suffered enough? Do I not suffer, every day, with every breath I take where he ignores me and refuses even to speak with me. Can he not let me apologise? I only want to assuage the hurt I know I caused him, that pain I see reflected in his eyes and the set of his jaw. I never meant to cause him this torment, and I ache to see him so angry and sullen. I believe he is worthy of so much more than I can give. Why won't he let me explain?" The memory of Hilarion's stiffening frame, the firm set of his eyes and the thin line of his unsmiling mouth brought another flood of tears.

Gisela heard the creak of hinges behind her. Heavy footfalls sounded on the floorboards as she bit her lip, controlling the rawness of her emotions with sheer willpower. With a hurried motion, she wiped her cheeks, pressing her fingertips against her eyelids and wiping away traces of her outpouring. Then she rose in one swift motion and hurried past the other person, eyes fixed on the ground. She heard them clear their throat and glanced up involuntarily.

The priest's round face and worried gaze brought a lump to her throat. His long, flowing cassock swept about him as he raised a hand, staying her attempt to slip past him. “What ails you, child?” he asked, his deep voice laden with concern.

Gisela shook her head, teeth sinking into soft lips, bringing pain to dispel the constriction in the back of her throat. “Nothing important, Elder.” She hesitated, then added, “I’m sorry for having concerned you needlessly.” Then she pulled free and ran out, allowing the downpour from the heavens to wash over her, hoping the cold and damp would pull her mind from the darkness of her thoughts.

9

Hilarion sat in the gloomy inn, half a mug of ale on the table before him. He stared out the door into the rain-streaked sky as he mulled over the look Gisela had given him after her practise session. *She wants to talk*, he thought. *What harm can it do?* The suppressed voice of his conscience piped up. *She deserves to suffer as much as I do for her inconsiderate words and childish outburst,* his practised outrage slammed back, unrelenting. *She has no right to come begging for forgiveness and asking for my understanding. She brought this on herself and should suffer for it.*

His hand balled into a fist on the tabletop as he tried with all his might to banish the sense of guilt that settled deep within him. *She deserves it!* he reiterated, as though doing so would help to dispel his unease. It did not. With a sigh, Hilarion grabbed the flagon and poured the remaining ale down his throat, belching as he stood and slammed the wooden vessel back onto the rough surface of the table. He flung his rifle over his shoulder, raised a hand in salute to the innkeep and strode out the door.

Hilarion had walked a few steps before his awareness fixed onto a bedraggled figure running across the green from the church. First, he took in the red fabric which clung to her legs, sodden through to a dark maroon. Heart pounding in his ears, Hilarion stopped short. Then he became aware of the curve of her shoulders, the way she held her arms crossed over her stomach even though it made running more clumsy.

Half of him wanted to go to her, clasp her to him and comfort her, while the other half remained stoic and impassive. As Hilarion warred with himself, the splashing steps from Gisela's trajectory across the village green changed to the pounding of footfalls on harder ground. Despite her awkward gait, she moved fast. It was only when she reached the alley beside the town hall, that Hilarion's better half won out.

"Gisela!" he called, his lethargy giving way to action. "Gisela, wait!"

The pounding rain drowned out his voice, and although he ran, he could not catch up with her. On the outskirts of the village, he pulled up short. He could not see Gisela's figure anymore. His hat streamed with water and mud sucked at his boots. Hilarion wiped the streaming liquid from his face, knowing the futility of the action even as he did it.

His attention was drawn away from the lane which Gisela must have taken. The sound of heavy footfalls approached along the main road, tugging at his awareness. Hilarion squinted into the distance, but could only hear the figure drawing nearer. His vision was almost entirely impaired by the driving, grey droplets cascading from above. *Horse*, he realised from the speed with which the approaching sound increased in volume, and stepped aside just as a rider appeared a few steps ahead of him.

The steed panicked at the unexpected sight of the man in the road, and rearing up in fright, it's hooves skidding in the slippery mud. The horse unseated its rider. The unfortunate horseman's cry of surprise was cut short by a squelch as he landed in a shower of mud. His mount pranced about in alarm and looked ready to bolt, but Hilarion stepped in, exuding an aura of calm, catching the reins in one hand and offering the other in appeasement. The horse was quick to soothe and allowed Hilarion to rub its waterlogged neck as he turned his attention to the man sitting in the mud.

"Are you all right, sir?" he asked, crossing the distance between them, the pacified equine following.

The man groaned as he looked upon himself all covered with dirt. Hilarion stretched out his other hand, which the unseated rider grabbed, pulling himself up while offering a grateful smile to the gamekeeper.

"Thank you, good man," he called out in a deep voice. "My body seems sound enough. No harm from the tumble, it would appear. Tell me, is there a village nearby? I travel with a hunting party, and we are looking for refuge from this storm."

Hilarion's pulse quickened and he hurried to say, "Why yes, milord. You are a few steps from Ylvaton. There is a good inn at the centre of the village, and I happen to be the gamekeeper in these parts, should your patron wish to hunt once the weather has cleared."

"Ah," the other replied. "What splendid news." He took up the reins and turned his mount back the way he had come. While Hilarion helped him back onto his mount, he asked, "What is your name?"

"Hilarion!" he shouted over the pounding of the rain.

"Have the inn prepare rooms for twenty men and you shall receive a worthy reward for your assistance today. For now, have my thanks." And with that, he disappeared back into the grey while Hilarion trudged towards the inn, all thoughts of Gisela wiped from his mind at the prospect of fulfilling his purpose and acting as a guide on a hunt.

10

Vincent woke with a groan. His mouth was dry. Chapped flakes stuck together on his parched lips. His throat burned, and as he opened his mouth to call for water, a hacking cough tore through him. His chest heaved with the force of his body's desire to expel phlegm. His head throbbed in complaint of the convulsions from his lungs, but the pain lightened to a dull ache once the cough subsided. Next, he became aware of the ache in his arms and legs.

His cough sparked a flurry of activity. Oskar came into view, overseeing half a dozen other people Vincent didn't recognise. A clammy cloth was applied to Vincent's forehead. Then strong arms lifted him into a sitting position, eliciting another moan as his muscles objected. Steam rose off a cup that a woman held up to his lips. He blinked twice, his mind unable to absorb what his eyes saw. Her warm smile was the only feature he registered, and it encouraged him to take wincing sips of the brew. It was bitter, but it did soothe the rawness in his throat. Once he finished drinking, he gingerly pushed himself into a resting position and drifted into darkness.

Vincent woke again to the sound of voices. One belonged to Oskar. It was unmistakable, but the other, a gruff, bass rumbling, was unfamiliar. Vincent tried to open his eyes, but they were gummed up with sleep. He wanted to roll over, rub his eyes and sit up, but his body refused. Aches constricted every movement. He blinked, freeing up one of his eyes, allowing him to get his bearings.

"Ah, y'er awake," the gravelly voice belonged to a short, rotund man with an air of authority about him. Vincent observed silver buttons on the coal-black coat as well as a stiff, white collar which came off the neck at an angle, jutting out above the shoulders. *Doctor,* Vincent thought as short fingers prodded him.

Words washed over Vincent, but his mind had a hard time grasping their meaning. As soon as he believed himself close to understanding, their significance slipped into obscurity again. The sheer effort exhausted him. The doctor patted Vincent's hand companionably and turned his words to Oskar, who stood nearby. Their voices drifted further away as Vincent allowed his body to sink into the stiff, white sheets—a bright whiteness to contrast the fuzzy darkness which enveloped him.

Sunlight streamed into the room, warming Vincent where he lay. His eyelids twitched. A late-summer breeze, laden with the scent of honeysuckle, brushed his cheek. The memory of a sweet dream twitched into a smile as his eyes opened. Vincent sat, his gaze travelling the expanse of a common sleeping room. A large silk screen stood at an angle. He imagined it had shielded him from view, but had been set aside to allow the sun in.

"Finally!" Oskar exclaimed. He strode over to Vincent's side. "You had me worried, old chap."

Vincent took a deep breath, and winced at the tenderness in his lungs and throat. "How long was I out for?" he murmured.

"Almost four days." When Vincent swung his legs over the side, Oskar stretched out an arm to check him. "The doctor says you should rest for a day after waking. You should eat, and you shall get as much sunlight and fresh air as possible. In the morning, you are permitted to begin walking about. He made it especially clear you should not overextend yourself and that you should keep clear of all dampness."

The gravity in Oskar's voice was unusual. Vincent looked up at his friend and decided to lighten the mood. "I've had enough dampness to last me a lifetime," he said, receiving a strained smile from his friend for his efforts. He continued, brightening even more. "I soaked up enough rain from that downpour to water all the king's horses for a year."

Oskar patted his hand, and Vincent turned his attention to the knitted blanket covering him. A patchwork of cheerful, coloured squares greeted him. The pain in his chest made itself known again, and it was soon followed by a short bout of coughing. Vincent was relieved, though. He felt so much better than he had the last time he woke.

Once the fit subsided, he flicked a glance at his friend again. "I expect my cover is blown," he murmured. It was half question, half statement, as though he dared to hope the assertion were false.

Oskar roused himself from his thoughts and laughed. The flash of hilarity in his eyes brought a smile to Vincent's lips. "In fact, I managed to get away with making you a lordling" came the light reply. A moment later, his features clouded over again as he added, "In all seriousness, Vincent, you had better write to your parents. I dared not. I was ready to face the music had you not awoken today. So, thank you, old sport, for saving my skin."

Vincent nodded. After a moment's thoughtful silence, he motioned with a quick gesture. A feather quill and parchment were proffered. They sat together, only the dutiful scratching of the nib breaking the stillness. With deliberate care, Vincent dipped the quill in an inkwell on a stand beside him. He took pleasure in this task, the like he had not performed in many weeks. It felt comfortable to write a letter. The actual act of allowing the script to form beneath his pen soothed him. It gave him the opportunity to keep his recriminations at bay.

He read his own words again, then folded the parchment twice. Oskar stepped forward, attentive as ever. "Allow me," he said, holding a candle to a stick of sealing wax. The crimson substance dripped onto the sheet, and then Vincent pressed his ring deep into the cooling mass. When he peeled it away, he revealed a rampant stag, sceptre in hand. Oskar extended an elegant hand. Vincent looked up from the mark on the seal. He nodded and handed the letter to his friend.

"That may not please them, but at least it will buy us some more time. Now I am officially convalescing in the countryside."

"I'll see to this and something to eat," Oskar said as he strode out of sight down a flight of rough-hewn stairs at the opposite end of the room.

11

Gisela squinted against the brightness of the blazing sky. She brushed a hand over her brow, wiping away droplets tickling her eyebrows. She lifted yet another leaf and peered at the bushel of grapes beneath. They were juicy and almost ripe, but her keen eye picked out one damaged by the recent storm. With a deft move, she plucked it, allowing it to fall into a basket at her feet.

"Gisela!" the rough voice jolted her away from the vine.

"Yes, father?"

"The shepherd hasn't returned yet. The sun is already low. Go and meet him. Help him if he's gone and lost another lamb. The meadows are treacherous with mud since the downpour."

"I'm almost done with this row. I'll finish it, and then I'll go up to the meadow."

"No, go now. I can finish up here."

Gisela nodded, brushing the sweat from her face once more. She set off at a brisk pace, following the narrow furrow sheep's hooves had carved into the scenery from their daily climb to the best pastures. She noted how, in some places, the well-worn path had changed shape. It formed a sharp gulley, sand washed away by the quantity of water that had spilled through the area a few days before. She stepped under the first trees, sighing with relief at the cool air as it soothed her scorched skin.

Her feet skipped out the steps to the traditional Landla dance. Upon noticing, she giggled. Her body always took over like that. No warning, just practised motion rolling forth. *Today would have been a dancing day*, she thought. A sigh escaped her lips. The longing seized her. Every day without music was a chore. All she wanted was to feel the lightness when the tune struck up. Spread her wings and rise up to float high above everything. She wanted to forget her cares.

"At least I haven't thought of *him* yet today," she murmured. *Hilarion. Ever-present gloom to darken a bright sunny day like today.* The unexpected strength of the storm brought panic to the farm. The consequences for the vineyard were the force guiding her family from dawn until dusk. There was nothing else more important than ensuring the grapes were fine. The memory of her father's worry filled her. As soon as the rain subsided, he had rushed out the house to check his fields for damage. The vineyard was his first stop, and his curses still rang in her ears.

The air temperature changed again. Warm sunlight greeted her. Warm, not hot. She glanced up at the soft, green grass, which swayed in a gentle breeze. Turning, she saw the sun slipping out of sight over the horizon. Then she heard the bleating of sheep. The flock came into sight at the top of a little knoll on the slope above her.

"Fred!" Gisela shouted, waving to the ten-year-old who floundered behind with a lamb in his arms.

"Oh, Gisela," he exclaimed. "It's broken a leg."

She cradled the fluffy creature to her breast and cooed in response to it's bleating.

"Thank you for coming up here," Fred chirped, a broad grin on his dirty face.

"Father sent me."

He nodded, and they walked in companionable silence. The sheep trotted ahead of them, the certainty of their destination driving them forward. The late-summer sunset bathed the path in pink light. By the time they reached the farmstead, the first stars twinkled in the deepening blue above them.

"Ah, you're back. I thought I might have to go out and fetch you." Sven sauntered over with a lantern swinging from his hand.

"Oh, good," Gisela flashed a smile at her brother. "Come and help me settle them for the night and see to this little one." Turning to Fred, she added, "Get yourself home. We don't want your mother aworrying."

"See ya!" the boy called as he clambered over the fence and hurried down the lane and out of sight. Gisela smiled after him.

"What happened to the lamb?" her brother's voice brought her back to the task at hand.

By the time they had seen to the chores and secured the injured creature's leg with a splint, night had fallen. Silver twinkles dotted the sky. Gisela paused on her way back to the house, absorbing their calm. *What would it be like to soar up there?* she wondered. *Float among the clouds to accompany the dragons.*

"Come along, Gise. There's a surprise for you!"

She whipped her head around, braids creating an arc about her. "What was that? What surprise?"

Sven laughed at the inquisitiveness in her voice. "Come on," was all he said.

Gisela trotted after him, reaching the threshold at the same time he did. Sven pushed the door, and it creaked on its hinges.

"Finally!" Robert exclaimed. "What took you so long?"

Gisela's gaze settled on her father sitting by the kitchen table in his usual place. He turned towards her, greeting her with a smile that shone bright in his cocoa eyes. "One of the lambs is injured, as you suspected, father."

He nodded, swallowing his food. "Never mind that now," he said at length. "Come and have your dinner, and then I'd like to discuss something with you."

A knot formed in Gisela's stomach, but she held her curiosity at bay. She slipped into her place at the table. The smell of fresh grape-leaf dolma had her stomach grumbling loud enough for both her brothers to burst out laughing. She laughed with them while she sat down. Together they ate the delectable dish. Gisela savoured the spices her mother had added to the meat filling.

"Gisela," her father began, once they had finished eating, and her mother cleared away the dishes together with Robert. Gisela met his gaze, eagerness burning in her eyes. "I have heard many compliments of your dancing," her father smiled. "At the crisis meeting this morning, many of our neighbours came to tell me what an honour it has been for them to attend your practise sessions."

"Why, thank you, Father. I'm glad they approve."

"You know, it is more than mere approval. They appreciate your talent. In just the past week, I have had three requests for your hand. I'm truly pleased the dancing has given you such opportunities."

Gisela's throat constricted. She felt cold and a little ill. Before she could say anything, her father added, "I was hoping you could show us tonight, so we might also share in your talent."

She blinked. At a loss for words, she choked out,

"Really?" Her mind was still struggling to come to grips with it all.

"You want me to wait all the way to the harvest festival?" he retorted with a mock pout. "You would make your father be the last to see, while everyone else goes in to town to gawk?"

"Oh, no, Father!" Gisela exclaimed. "You don't need to worry about that. I'll gladly share this with you." She felt a rising uncertainty about marriage proposals. Somehow, she'd always known it would come, but now that this stage in her life was here, she felt terrified of it. She cleared her throat and ventured, "Father, who has asked for my hand?"

"I'll tell you when I've chosen your husband," he said. "No need to think about it yet. I'll make a decision after the festival. Who knows, I might get better offers yet."

Gisela swallowed, then pushed despite the tremor in her voice, "And how will you choose who is suitable?"

Her father shook his head. "So many questions, sweetheart. I'll choose whoever proves best capable of providing for you. I'll have to gauge standard of living and such like."

No thought of love, she thought, but refrained from actually commenting.

Robert gestured her over to a space that had been cleared beside the fireplace in the living area. Sven pulled a large object out from a shadowy corner. A musical note emanated from the item, eliciting a gasp from Gisela.

"Is that an accordion?"

Sven grinned at her as he handed the instrument to their father.

What? Gisela thought. *Father plays the accordion? I must be dreaming. Please don't let it turn into a nightmare.*

Notes streamed out from under her father's rough fingertips and Gisela pushed all thoughts other than dance from her mind. The melody drew her in and Gisela's worries lifted from her shoulders. She gave way to the tune. Her feet floated over the floor, light and precise in every motion, and she was transported to a time long past when the sight of her father playing the accordion was familiar. Memories of music and laughter, the smell of her mother's cooking and the sight of her father playing and singing surged within her. As Gisela danced, she also remembered her love of dancing came from this place—this very room. Throughout the winters, music had filled the farmhouse, keeping the howling snow-laden winds at bay.

What happened? Why did things change? What made father turn against music and dancing?

12

Leaves rustled in the verdant canopy above Hilarion. He listened to the sweet call of the birds as he trod a well-used game path. A loose pebble caught his eye. He flicked it off the path with the toe of his boot, then continued on his way. A branch hung low, cutting into the path a little above head-height. Hilarion dropped a satchel from his shoulder and pulled forth a saw.

A loud crack, followed by a snapping crash, tore through the forest as the heavy branch tumbled to the earth. It came to rest across the path with a resounding thud. Brushing sweat from his brow, Hilarion wiped the saw clean before returning it to its place. He stood to one side and took a swig from a water flask, which he subsequently returned to a pouch attached to his belt. With a sigh, Hilarion went to work on the branch, tugging it and hefting until it slipped into the undergrowth beside the path.

He gave a satisfied grunt, swung his satchel back into place and continued up the trail, his eyes roving. A jauntiness came into his step, and he began to whistle a folk tune—echoing the birds' chirping. He noted with satisfaction that the weights, which had dragged his heart down into the mire, were lighter. Serving a purpose—feeling useful—had swept away his resentment, just like an autumn wind did the leaves.

This hunt will be the best, most successful entertainment this lord has ever had, and I shall prove my worth.

All day, Hilarion traipsed through the woods. The work of cleaning and pruning back in preparation of the hunt kept his mind off Gisela. It was a taste of freedom he savoured. Tending to his duty and his own work was a breath of fresh air.

Bless that young lord and bless the rain, he thought. For had it not been for the downpour, the hunting party would surely have passed by Ylvaton without a backward glance, and Hilarion would never have been granted this opportunity. He smiled, a true signifier of his deep joy. It smouldered in his eyes—igniting a fire he thought long extinguished. *What a fine day, and fabulous moment, where all things come together perfectly.*

The following day, Hilarion took an early morning walk through a different section of the forest, continuing his work. The sun rose high in the sky, and at noon, with a rumbling belly, he headed out of the trees. He smiled and waved at a farmer and his family who were working hard in their vineyard. Their baffled looks and half-hearted waves brought a rolling surge of merriment, the like of which had not crossed Hilarion's lips in over a decade.

He stopped. Laughter. To laugh. Where had this change come from? After so much time, hilarity seemed raw. He tested it again, recalling the family's looks of surprise and feeling the joyful response. With the laughter came a lightness to his heart. It leapt into the sky, soaring above him under a golden, summer sun. Another tune came to his lips and his gait matched its light-heartedness. Hilarion brushed a hand over the leaves of a hedge, felt the tingling of life at his fingertips. The force of all things growing fizzed within him, eliciting another laugh—for the pure delight of being alive.

Red roof tiles glowed in the mid-afternoon, inviting Hilarion into the cool of sheltered buildings. He stepped inside the inn, grateful for the protective shade. His arms tingled in relief at the contrast in temperature.

"Ah, gamekeeper!" the thick-set innkeep called from under his thick beard. "The usual?" It was not so much a question as a confirmation. He did not wait for Hilarion's deliberate nod, but turned to dish up the day's stew. As the fragrant victuals were being ladled into a carved, wooden bowl, Hilarion spied an empty bench and headed towards it. His trajectory was interrupted by a thin man of middling stature. Hilarion squinted at him. Then his memory superimposed another image of this man, waterlogged and coated in mud.

"Well-met, gamekeeper," the stranger said, inclining his head.

"Indeed," Hilarion replied, his mouth twitching upward. "I'm glad to see you well since our last meeting." The man frowned and Hilarion hurried to add, "No offense meant, sir. I come to inform you, and your lord, that all is in order. A hunt can commence whenever he wishes."

The other raised his hands, an apologetic smile creasing his features. "His Lordship has been taken ill. I do not know whether he cares to set forth on a hunt. You will have to bide your time. I'll have someone send for you should your services be required." Hilarion shrugged, biting back his disappointment. The man added, "For your help the other day." He pulled a small leather pouch from his pocket and handed it to Hilarion. Then the man turned and hurried up the stairs.

Cupping the clinking pouch in his hand, Hilarion smiled. He made his way to his seat where he emptied the contents of the leather bag and counted the thick, silver coins. After tucking the purse into his pocket, Hilarion turned his attention to the bowl of stew, which wafted its steamy scent towards him. He savoured every bite, marvelling at the fragrant harmony the innkeeper's wife called forth from simple potatoes and carrots.

13

"I'm satisfied with ye," the doctor rumbled in his deep voice.

Vincent nodded, "Yes, the cough is much better... but shouldn't I spend more time indoors? I mean... I am ill, after all."

"What ye should 'ave done is stay outta the rain. Delicate constitutions shouldna spend hours riding in a downpour. It's no wonder y'er ill, sir," came the forceful reply. "Now, fresh air, good sunlight, healthy food and a dash o' exercise will be yer cures. Begone with ye!"

Vincent stiffened. The older man was already halfway out the room. Vincent's hand clenched as his mother's sharp voice echoed in his mind. *You cannot expect them to understand. They are uncouth by nature. It is our duty to guide them, to mould their actions. We are the sun, which provides them the light they need to grow.*

Vincent swung his legs over the edge of the bed. *How is it, this "uncouth" doctor can be so certain of himself?* he thought. *One of them has to be wrong.*

His mother affirmed over and over her belief in the common classes' depravity and ignorance. She also recoiled from them. Vincent knew she blamed peasants for his brother's fatal illness. *They are always crawling with vermin,* she had said once. *When they live with the sickness all around them, it does not show. Then they spend their time spreading diseases wherever they go.* Nevertheless, his journey had shown him enough sickness among the common people to know his mother's beliefs were warped. *And they are only more so because of Albert's death,* he thought.

Vincent felt his shoulder's drooping. He took a deliberate deep breath, steadying his thoughts. *I know Mother is not right about everything. Perhaps it is time to trust this doctor and do as he says.* Not following his mother's advice was something new, an act to be savoured. Vincent smiled to himself as he strode across the room to a sunny patch beside an open window. He glanced out and noted the beginnings of a crowd gathering on the village green below. *Time to test this doctor's remedy and get a feel for simple village life*, he thought, watching the ant hive of browns and greys and listening to the excited chatter floating on the breeze.

"Ah, there you are!"

Vincent smiled, but did not look up from his study of the local populace where they gathered. "Yes, Oskar.

The doctor said I should make the most of sunlight and fresh air. I do not yet feel up to gallivanting about, which he also prescribes. This seems as good a place as any to continue my recovery, don't you think?"

Oskar nodded, his gaze traversing the window, curious about what held Vincent's attention. "I wonder what they're up to," he mused.

"It looks like some form of celebration."

They watched as a group of adolescent women came into view beyond the crowd. "Dancers," Oskar said. "The innkeep mentioned something about the rehearsal for the harvest festival. I never thought it would draw a crowd."

Vincent rose and pushed open the window, breathing in the flower-scented breeze as it rustled over him. His attention was drawn back out beyond the crowd by movement. The young women were moving in silence for he could not hear the music. Only a few notes drifted to him where he now perched on the windowsill. Vincent did not sense the rough wood under his fingers. He barely heard Oskar gasp as he drew up beside Vincent. All things were forgotten. All things save the one, which had deftly nabbed his attention and now reeled it in.

The girl with the crimson skirt, who took pride of place at the centre of the troupe, danced meadow flowers. Vincent didn't know how her movements could elicit such imagery, but the grace of her body caressed his mind with a whole range of pictures. Eyes blind to all else, Vincent absorbed every detail. Meadow flowers turned into swaying trees, bowing before the wind, followed by the rushing caper of a brook over mossy stones. Next, she whirled and leapt, and in that instant, she ceased to be a creature of the earth as she launched into the sky, her arms became wings, rising above, extending beyond the reach of earthly gravitas. Then she alighted again, her feet sinking into the sturdy foundation of the mountains. On it went, each motion conjuring an image so powerful Vincent sensed the presence of these creatures and places more deeply than the earth, which was his home.

Beautiful, he thought. The woman performing in the distance below was more than that, but his mind stumbled to find a better word. *Grace, delight, elegance...* beauty resonated best. Her dance was like nothing he had ever seen before—pure and intense and meaningful. Meaning. It was this that reeled Vincent in, but unlike a fish on a hook, he did not struggle. He yielded without a second thought. The girl who wore red (that mark of nobility, shade of life's-blood, colour of the disk of sustenance as it rose from the ashes of night) was everything to him—sun and moon and sky, all invigorating life-forces combined into a single, human form.

Motion ceased. Only the fabric of the skirt whipped about her legs in what remained of the breeze of her passionate dance. A mantle of profound silence settled over all who watched. Vincent could not help but succumb to the melancholy in the folds of that cloak. *Why did it have to end?* A sigh parted his lips, and a sweet, fresh breath of life poured into his lungs. He could not remember a time when air had felt so bountiful. *How long did I hold my breath?* he wondered.

Beside him, Oskar stirred, and below them, verdure became visible again as the crowd dispersed, voices carrying on the air.

Oskar, too, sucked in a breath, and after a brief pause, collecting his scattered thoughts, he said, "Now that, you don't see every day."

Vincent held his own council, turning his thoughts to the spectacle he just witnessed. He glanced out the window and observed a swish of crimson striding with purposeful steps right across the green space stretched out before him.

"She is beautiful," Oskar breathed. "I wonder—"

Vincent's eyes narrowed and he snapped his attention fully upon his friend. "No," he cut in, silencing the other man. "You will not do any of the myriad dirty things playing in that horrid little mind of yours. No. She is not for the likes of you, nor ever will be, and you will keep well away from her." Vincent spoke with authority. His proscription carried a weight that frightened him a little. Vincent licked his lips, his eyes breaking contact, only to flick back into his friend's gaze. *A little harsh.* The thought flashed through his mind.

Before Vincent could contemplate the nature of his

response or the vehemence in his voice, Oskar bowed. Everything about his stance radiated deference. "As you wish, my—"

Vincent laid a hand on the taller man's shoulder. Their gazes met, and both nodded a curt acknowledgement of the other. "We need speak of it no more," Vincent resolved. "However, I have need of those simple garments we used in Averly."

Soon afterwards, he emerged from the inn wearing a plain brown shirt and breeches. His appearance was so nondescript, no one in the inn noticed his departure, as patrons gushed their rapture for the afternoon's spectacle. Without a backward glance, Vincent strode forward towards the church. His heart quickened pace. The question, *what am I doing?* shimmered at the edges of his conscious mind, but the bubble of his curiosity and desire rose even faster, extinguishing the thought in its infancy.

Pushing the door, Vincent stepped inside, momentarily blinded by the dimness of the place. He was comforted by the uniformity of churches. Although this building was smaller than the great cathedral in the capital, and larger than the family chapel he frequented most, it was the same in all its essential aspects. Wooden pews faced a stone altar, which shone in the brilliant, colourful light of stained-glass windows. Brightly painted images adorned the walls. He recognised the mother in one and the father in another. The separated aspects of the Dragon Lords:

shimmering scales and life-giving breath depicted as tongues of sunlight.

Vincent's gaze fell upon the kneeling figure of a woman. She was the only living being there, other than himself. He stepped forward as he took in the shade of her elaborate, free-flowing skirt spread across the dark wood of the floor. Her oval face was upturned to an effigy of the Sacred Heart. *A profile worthy of a goddess*, he thought, his eyes roving over the cascading ebony of her hair. He stood, frozen in place, as she knelt in prayer.

At first, it was a tickle in the back of his throat. Vincent's preoccupied mind ignored it entirely. Then, a violent convulsion heaved through his chest, pain constricting his lungs. His eyes burned, his rib cage strained against the force of his cough, and Vincent struggled for air, gasping like a fish out of water.

14

Startled at the sound, Gisela turned and came to her feet in a single swift motion. Her heart sped up to beat at the thrumming rhythm of a jive, and her doe eyes flared wide. What she saw was a man, bent double, as his body tried to expel his lungs. She moved before any thought formulated in her mind. His need for assistance was clear. He could barely stand from the force of his cough. She reached him and steadied him, supporting his elbow. He looked up, dark eyes rimmed red, and nodded at her as he drew a ragged breath before the next fit broke out.

"Sit here," she said, gesturing towards the nearest pew. The hacking sounds calmed enough for the two steps it took them. Once seated, though, the irritation in his throat resumed his plight, and Gisela watched for a moment, hands falling to her sides. *What can I do?*

The man leaned back, drawing breath again, and

Gisela's gaze fell onto his exposed throat, just above the v-shape created by his shirt. Her mother's fail-safe remedy to still the tickling of an irritating cough popped into her mind, and without thinking, Gisela leaned forward. Her fingers lightly touched the soft hollow between the man's collar bones. His gaze snapped up, locking onto her. An electric tingle travelled up her arm to her elbow. Taking a breath to steady herself, Gisela maintained the contact, consciously thinking, *This will help. That is what is important.*

She trembled under his unwavering gaze. He was clearly shocked, and Gisela swallowed against the dryness that swept through her mouth. She licked her lips. Knowing she needed to keep her finger on the pressure point, Gisela struggled with the proximity to an unknown person. Her breathing quickened under the intensity of his bright eyes. He had fine features, with high cheekbones and a prominent nose. His full lips caught her attention as she noticed his breathing settle. Her eyes flicked back to his, and his shock washed over her even more pronounced than before. Gisela strained to keep her finger in the hollow of his throat. She knew if she did not, his affliction would return.

She dropped her gaze and murmured, "Mother says this is the best way to stop a coughing fit. I apologize for being so forward."

The man cleared his throat and raised his arm. His

hand brushed hers as he placed his own finger in the hollow. She withdrew her hand in the swift motion of someone being stung and stepped back. The distance helped, but still she felt uncomfortable. She studied the intense shine of his black boots as she searched for something to say. *Water.* The thought popped into her head. Relieved at the opportunity to break the awkward moment, Gisela spun around, hurrying to the priest's alcove. She knocked on the wooden door. When there was no reply, she pushed it inward with a heavy creak.

"Elder," she called. Only silence answered her. Identifying a small wooden cup beside a clay pitcher, Gisela stepped into the even cooler windowless room. The chill of the air contrasted noticeably with the heat on her arms. Gisela paused, becoming aware of how flushed she felt. Heat coursed through her. It roiled in her abdomen and flared in her chest. *What is this?* She had to steel herself against the tremble in her hand,which caused a drop to spill from the pitcher. Her awareness focused on the liquid as it splashed onto the toe of her boot. Gisela drew breath, trying to calm her agitated nerves. *Whatever is the matter with me?* She wondered as she hurried back to the man, all her attention focused on keeping water in the cup she held.

"Thank you." His voice was harsh from the irritated throat, and yet not unpleasant. Gisela stiffened at the renewed hot flush that tore through her when his fingers brushed hers as she passed him the cup. Red fabric crumpled under her fist as she turned, but the man's free hand rose to the crook of her arm, staying her departure.

"Please, Miss. What is your name?"

All sound died in her throat. Her body wanted to draw closer to this man, and it took all her might to fight the impulse. She stepped back, knocking into the pew behind her. Her lungs craved air again. *Why do I keep forgetting to breathe?*

With her tongue, Gisela moistened her lips. Words eluded her. Her gaze flicked up to his as he peered at her over the cup. Gisela glanced away again. *I'm behaving like a dunce.* Breath rattled through her, forced consciously, but it did not help to clear her mind.

The cup scraped against the pew as he set it down. "Well, perhaps it is only right I should introduce myself first. You are absolutely right, Miss. It is the proper way to do things." He nodded and said, "My name is Albert." Then he paused again, hesitating. His eyes turned serious, but then a smile crept onto his face. Gisela was flooded with his kindness. It sent a renewed tingling sensation through her. Despite herself, she leaned forward.

Flustered once more by the realisation of her actions, Gisela straightened. Her voice strained, but she was able to choke out her name and bid him good afternoon. Then she hastened from that place, her face burning. She swirled past another man, tall and robust, sporting muscles that reminded her of the rippling mass of mountains gracing the horizon beyond the church door. She kept her gaze steeled on the ground to avoid eye contact with this other stranger and rushed out into the warm afternoon. Skirts billowed out on the breeze, whirling as the flushed heat did within her—swirling along with the confused thoughts in her mind.

A shadow stepped away from the church wall and into her path. Disoriented as she was, it took Gisela a moment to notice the motion. "What was that all about?" Hilarion asked, and Gisela detected strain in his voice.

Her heart, which had fluttered in her throat before, now plummeted into the deepest recess of her stomach. Gisela gasped in her surprise. *Can this day get any worse?* With the edges of her mind, she tried to force her body to cooperate with her. A second breath stilled the agitated confusion gripping her since she first came into contact with the man in the church. In this instant, however, her mind latched onto something better—an emotion she could master.

"Now you want to talk?" she accused. "You've been arsey with me for weeks and now, suddenly, you want to speak? I have nothing left to say to you, Hilarion."

She swept past him, but his hand caught her. His rough and calloused touch brushed the crook of her elbow in the same place, but this contact only brought on greater contempt and irritation. Though before she could vent her growing anger, Hilarion spoke. "What did the stranger want?"

"That is none of your business," she retorted, and smiled her satisfaction when he flinched at the bite in her tone.

"Of course it is," he insisted, anger flashing from the depths beneath his hat. "He is a stranger. You have no business talking with him."

Gisela's eyebrows arched into her forehead. "You would criticize a man for giving his thanks when he was assisted, briefly during a coughing fit? What is wrong with you?" She jerked her arm out of his grasp, shaking her head in disbelief. "What is your problem?"

"I care for you, Gisela. I don't want you to fall victim to vile gossip."

"Oh, so you're jealous? Because I gave a man some water when he needed it? You've lost your marbles!"

"Perhaps," he exclaimed, "but only because I'm madly in love with you, Gisela."

She rounded on him then, her shoulders squared as she lowered her voice. "When I wanted to apologise, because I knew my reaction that day caused you pain and that was never my intention... when I wanted to apologise, you refused to come near me. Well, now, I have moved beyond that. Our friendship died when you did not respect it enough to admit that you wished for more than just friendship. Our friendship died when you refused to take my feelings into account. All you ever think about is yourself. You never gave a toss about me, only about how I made you feel."

"How dare you?" Hilarion interjected. "I have always thought of you, of what is best for you. I wanted what you want, but you are too much of a spoilt brat to even see it."

Gisela laughed. It was harsh, condescending. "No. You took pity on me and thought I was easy pickings because I was always alone. You thought you could befriend me and then make me feel indebted to you. As though I owed you something for your kindness and your friendship. Although, you only sought me out because I helped you lighten your own burden." Her eyes narrowed as she rasped, "But, that's not how this works. Friendship needs mutual respect, not one person being beholden to the other. And let's not even begin with marriage!"

Hilarion stared at her. She could see he was searching for a retort, but Gisela headed him off. Poking her finger into his chest, she added, "I owe you nothing. Nothing!"

Then she turned and ran in a flurry of crimson fabric and ebony tresses. *Why does he always make it so hard to be nice to him? Why does he always push everyone away? Now I've just gone and made things worse. And he's going to resent me even more for it. Dragons, he makes me so angry!*

15

Vincent sat in the cool of the church. His thoughts wheeled through an intricate web—ever down and into the dark. There was light though. Or colour, to be more specific, although the black thoughts kept reclaiming him. Why, oh why had he given her that name? Vincent spooled back time in his mind, returning to his question. *What is your name?* And he relived her confusion, uncertainty and the hesitation that swirled in her beautiful brown eyes. Everything about her exuded insecurity, and he fought with his urge to gather her into his arms and whisper to her that he would keep her safe. Instead, he decided to change tack. *Well, perhaps it is only right I should introduce myself first.*

When the words left his mouth, a hasty, half-formed thought flashed through his mind. *I cannot reveal my real name. I have to keep this secret.* In his haste to dissimulate his own identity, Vincent donned the cape of one who was ever present in his mind. *Why Albert? Of all the infuriating names I could have chosen, why his?* He knew the answer to that question. It had lain dormant with him for many years. *I chose it because I cannot escape who I am. Albert created me.* Vincent allowed his head to sink into his hands. He embraced the darkness, which mirrored the absence of light in his own heart—and he thought on death then.

Brother, he called in the shadows of his mind. *Brother, why did you leave us?*

Did he leave, or was he taken away? A small voice piped up. Vincent swatted at it, as though it could be induced to fly away like a pesky insect.

Albert, Mother misses you so terribly. She speaks of everything else, anything else, only not of you. Although we all know you are what is in her mind. She pours all her worry onto me now. She has become ever so protective. Terrified, I'd say. I think I broke her heart when I left on this journey. What kind of sons are we? To break our mother's heart so? She clings to you with the flood of all she says, all the words that speak nothings. She makes your absence present at all times by refusing to speak of you, but always implying what could have been had you not left—been taken away.

Vincent swallowed hard. His throat pained him, but it was emotion, not illness which caused the constriction. His mind plunged further, onto the next downward revolution.

Father... Father is a different man since you were taken from us. You would not recognise him. The laughter left his eyes. You took that with you, Albert. And because the light is gone, he cannot see the colours of the universe anymore. Everything is grey because you aren't in his vision. Everything is compared to you, Albert, and he always finds something wanting. Nothing and no one can measure up to you in the measuring stick of father's mind. We are all worthless, meaningless—nothing.

Catherine. She despises me. I see her constant appraisal, ever-present comparison of me to you. She disapproves of me because I am not you. They all say she will make a marvellous queen, but what about my heart? Her heart, for that matter. What about us? And Madeleine? Why should she suffer so? How could you leave us all? Why did your passing break everything? The whole place is a mess, just because one person snuffed out. Catherine is my ever-present reminder that anyone who isn't you, just isn't good enough.

"And me?" Vincent croaked aloud as his mind took the next rotation down into the deep. *Where have you left me? With two broken parents, the woman who loves you, and a set of shoes the size of sailing ships that no man could ever fill... Mother looks at me with the terror of her loss. Father sees past me, through me. Catherine despises me. I am a shadow beside your larger-than-life, more-colourful-than-rainbows existence, which has taken on a life of its own. That's why I had to escape. I fled the coop as soon as I had the chance, only to fall prey to your hounding again. Now she will call me by your name. She—Gisela. I cannot bear the thought.*

Colour overwhelmed the darkness. It began with the first tantalising swirl of strawberry red, leading the way for a host of bright shades and many hues. The colours in the embroidery of her bodice. Sunlight streaming down onto a stage of whirling dancers, each skirt a different dab of colour to wash away the blackness—colourlessness left behind by death. Now life brought its own palette. Gisela was life, Albert, death, and yet, by some secret twisting of fate, Vincent knew his choice of alias was giving the name Albert a new lease on life. *It is well*, he thought, his chest expanding in the calm serenity of breath, *I shall give you life again, Albert. Just this once. But I don't do it for you. This, I shall do for myself.*

As his hands fell away, Vincent noticed they were damp. He looked down at them, surprised. Fingertips travelled back to his cheeks where sticky trails left their marks. He laughed. It was loud and filled with exuberance, and a hint of surprise. "I cried," he murmured as inner calm returned, the weight of the thought sinking it to the depths of a crystal lake whose ripples soon stilled.

Vincent rose. He stretched, noticing the cobwebs from years of living a half life whisk away on the breeze of a spring cleaning. It was a good day. He met Gisela, the beautiful dancer, and thoughts of her confusion lit a flame in his heart. It smouldered like nothing else he'd ever experienced. The coldness clutching his heart was swept away in a whirl of her blazing, fiery skirts while her large, brown eyes dragged him into a new, warm place. Vincent was a changed man, and he knew it.

16

Gisela spent the next few days working hard. She flung herself into the toils of the vineyard, preparing for the harvest. The renewed strength of the sun ripened the fruit fast and soon the greatest task of all would be upon them. Although Gisela was known to be hard-working, her mother commented on several occasions about this new-found zeal for questions regarding the harvest. She threw herself into the tasks her father set. She became engrossed by her activities. She kept herself busy from the moment her eyes fluttered open with the first rays of sunlight until her lids fell closed from exhaustion when she lay down at night.

Tiring herself out was deliberate. Gisela did everything she could to keep her thoughts away from a certain young man she met in church. When she found her mind straying back to the encounter, an unfamiliar flame ignited in her belly. Gisela made her actions more pronounced, focusing all her attention on what she was doing. She knew she had to. Self-preservation demanded it, for although she did not know precisely what her physical reactions to that man meant, she knew enough to fear her impulses. The terrifying road that stretched out from that encounter beckoned to her constantly, but she maintained a front of dignity as she refused to look down the path of enticing possibility. She would resist. She had to.

Gisela's trepidation grew when she accompanied her family to church, as she always did on holy days. As the weekly journey drew near, Gisela's insecurities grew. Could she set foot in that place and still keep the memories of that man at bay? Would she give away her terrifying secret? Would the people of her village see the flame that burned within her, which consumed her every waking moment? She knew she had to remain calm, but she feared she didn't know how.

Following her father into the enclosed coolness, Gisela steeled her eyes onto the colourful glass at the extreme of the church. Her head never turned as she passed the place where a lighting bolt had kindled her desire. The only sign of the memory was a tingling sensation travelling from her right fingertip to her elbow. *Focus on breath.* In it went, and her chest rose. Then out came the air, and her vision cleared again. Light danced across the floor in blue and red and green and gold. She watched the display as she settled onto the hard, wooden bench beside her brother, Robert. He chatted to someone behind them, but Gisela only felt the outpouring of his words while she pulled her attention to the coloured smudges of light on the wooden flooring.

Silence descended on the congregation. Gisela felt her brother tugging her upward. It was only then she saw everyone was standing. Quiet curiosity had some straining their necks to get a better view. Of what, Gisela knew not, nor did she care—or so she thought. When the tall man walked into view though, she gasped at his silken finery. His short, brown cloak swayed about his shoulders, shimmering in the dull light. As he turned to greet her father with a pleasant smile, her eyes picked out a gleaming russet lining. His doublet was the same shade of brown as the cloak. Although there was no embroidery or brocade in his outfit, the quality of the materials used were unlike anything Gisela had ever seen before. They screamed of wealth and power.

Who is this man? she wondered. Gisela had heard the rumours when he and his retinue lodged at the inn. News like that always travelled like wildfire. Their lands belonged to the king, so there were few lords to ever come into the vicinity. Any lords or barons passing by usually stayed in neighbouring Huton by the River. She remembered once seeing a lord when she accompanied her father to dispatch their wine barrels, and the outfit on that occasion had been garish, pompous and overbearing. *Each person is different, with their own tastes,* she thought.

Returning to the present moment, Gisela noted the family seated in the first row scuttling out to make room for the lord. He flicked his head in their direction, acknowledging their action, and took his place at the front. In the rustling commotion that followed, while everyone resumed their seats, Gisela glanced about at the other men accompanying the lord. She was surprised and relieved she could not locate the man she helped a few days earlier. Just the memory of his touch on her arm brought back the blossoming glow in her abdomen, and she was forced to breathe deeply to steady her increasing heart-rate.

Gisela was grateful when the priest took up his position at the pulpit. She focused her attention on the gilded dragon winding its way up the base of the stand upon which he rested an enormous tome. She loved the tales of the Dragon Gods and their work to bring peace and prosperity to humans. As the priest's words flowed over her, she was transported into another plane, to where the Dragons, *praised be their endeavours*, brought the light of insight to humans and gave the king custodianship of the land. It was one of her favourite stories, but she wondered whether the priest deliberately selected it because this lord was in attendance. She knew the priest preferred more obscure passages for the benefit of his congregation.

As soon as the sermon ended, the lord rose to

stride out again. Gisela observed his gaze roving over the assembled villagers without actually making contact. He looked over them, his indifference palpable. She felt herself stiffen—bristle, even—at the thought that the priest's sermon fell on deaf ears. This man cared nothing for the people. He was unconcerned with their plight or his duty towards them. He enjoyed his status without acknowledging his role as benefactor. *Then again,* she thought, *he isn't our lord. He is just passing through. Convalescing after an illness brought on by being caught out in that horrendous storm. Perhaps his haughtiness is due to a lack of connection. And why would he show any interest in us if he is only passing through? At least, he isn't our king, gods be blessed. Having such a man as ruler would undoubtedly undo everything the dragons ever created for us.* Noticing the tension in her muscles, Gisela relaxed again, giving the man the benefit of the doubt.

She left the church together with her family and allowed her father to steer them away without giving them time to gawk at the lord and his retinue striding over to waiting horses. The only curiosity Gisela allowed herself was wondering whether the lord was leaving or just going on a ride in the hills.

17

Hilarion stood under the eaves of the inn. He watched as the villagers spilled out of the church behind the stranger in the cloak that shimmered in the bright sunlight. By the lord's side, Hilarion made out the man he had spoken to about going hunting. Their heads were bowed in conversation. Then, the man spun around and hurried out of sight behind the inn. Hilarion turned his attention back to the lord who stood and waited, but then his mind was drawn towards another group as they descended the two steps from the church door.

Three tall men accompanied by a dumpy woman, and behind them, grace personified. Gisela's finest frock was dark blue, bringing out the shade of her complexion to perfection. He noted a bemused smile flit across her lips and saw her glance at the antics of some villagers straining to see what the lord and his escort would do. Hilarion drank in the sight of Gisela's slim figure, her long braids dancing about her shoulders as she moved. It surprised him that she did not spare a second glance for the fine lord or the men with him. He wondered whether he had treated her unfairly when they spoke last.

Am I overbearing and jealous? he questioned. *Was I overreacting?* He thought back on the scene he observed a few days before. Gisela's shy smile, the other man's hand touching her arm. Being too far away, he did not hear what they said, but in hindsight, he thought it was possible he misinterpreted. *She had every right to be angry with me then*, he conceded. *I was most insensitive.*

The clip-clop of hooves brought Hilarion's attention back to the present. Realising the horses being brought forward were intended for the lord and his following, Hilarion sidled to the group of riders as they mounted up. He pulled his hat from his head, twisting it between his hands, waiting and wondering whether there would even be an opportune moment to speak with the man he rested his hopes on. When the stable hands stepped away, Hilarion realised his chance was slipping from his grasp. He took a brusque step towards the lord's cloudy mount and cleared his throat.

The grey beast tossed its head, forcing Hilarion to take a step back. He sensed the rider's irritation in the creature's agitation and wondered whether he was ruining any chance he might have had. *It's too late now for doubts*, he chided as he looked up with all the determination he could muster.

"Excuse my boldness, my lord," he stated. "I wish only to inform you, sir, that the forests are full with game, and the paths are tended to. I have personally overseen all is prepared should you wish to go on a hunt."

The man stared at him with a haughty expression and nodded. "I shall send for you when the desire strikes," he affirmed, flicking his fingers in Hilarion's direction. The furrow, a semi-permanent feature of the gamekeeper's brow, deepened as his face darkened. The round dismissal was demeaning, and it stung. The muscles in his jaw strained from the force of his clenching. Hilarion turned and came face-to-face with the man he originally met during the downpour.

"How dare you approach his lordship so?" the man's voice was incredulous. "Have you no respect for your betters?"

Hilarion forced an apology through his gritted teeth and left. He spent the remainder of his day rethinking all the years he had yearned for this moment, an opportunity to do his work and receive praise for it, but instead, he found the time spent without snobbish lordlings prancing about was his actual blessing. *I'll go back to my days of peaceful wandering in the forest and trapping the animals to avoid overpopulation, and I will never complain about my lot again,* he promised.

18

Vincent was overcome by a surge of guilt as his horse trotted away from the short man. He had seen the insult in the proud gamekeeper's face, and Vincent wished it could have been different. *It is necessary*, he reminded himself, swallowing the bitterness. He would continue to put on the act of the selfish, indifferent aristocrat. He did not want the good folk of Ylvaton to see through his ruse, and changing nothing more than his outfit would not keep the astute fooled for long.

Oskar rode up beside him. "You make a priceless swaggerer, Vincent," he laughed. "I haven't had this much fun in aeons."

Vincent felt his cheeks crease into a smile despite himself. "I am glad for the opportunity to entertain you, dear friend." After a brief pause, he added, "And if it means I can get to know the lovely Gisela better, then it will prove well worthwhile."

"We are going to need a reasonable alibi if we are to stay in this dump much longer."

Now Vincent grinned, his pearly teeth flashing. "I think the good gamekeeper has given us the perfect reason to stay for several weeks and escape suspicion entirely. Since I informed my parents I would stay here to convalesce, they, too will not expect me home in the near future."

"What?" Oskar exclaimed, "You're going hunting? Actually, hunt?"

"Yes. Why-ever not?"

Oskar threw his hands up, as he chuckled, "You're as keen as mustard for this bird." He shook his head, a knowing glint smouldering in his eyes. Vincent arched an eyebrow by way of reply. "You are lost!" Oskar exclaimed and winked a devilish grin spreading over his face. "I promise I'll keep my paws where you can see them," he added, wiggling his eyebrows.

"You can drop your lecherous insinuations. My intentions are quite honourable."

"Of course they are," Oskar retorted, his tone oozing sarcasm.

Vincent whipped the reins into the air before him. His jaw clenched as he bit back the angry tirade flitting into his mind. Instead of replying, Vincent turned to his retinue, which thundered up behind them. Oskar threw back his head, laughed and, with a sparkle in his eye, exclaimed so the others in their party could hear, "Hunting it is then. As you wish, my lord!"

A few days later, Vincent returned from a walk about the town in his disguise as Albert. He was only accompanied by his personal guard. He enjoyed the peaceful time spent walking cobbled streets, gazing up at the varied sizes with their yellow-brown brick walls. Dogs barked at his passing and the odd hog snuffled around in the gutter. The two men rounded the corner of the mayor's home, walking side by side like friends, when Vincent stopped short. His gaze traversed the crowd gathering on the village green. The hairs on his arms prickled at the mounting intensity shimmering in the air. He could almost hear a hum of excitement—the undercurrent thrilling beneath the hubbub of fifty-or-so people talking, murmuring their anticipation.

Vincent turned to the moustached man beside him. A curt nod and a glance was the extent of their exchange. Then Vincent pushed his hands deep into the pockets of his breeches, and the other man sidled up to the tavern where he took up his position, leaning against the wall with a nonchalant air disguising the piercing nature of his gaze. Vincent observed his companion before he slipped into the crowd on his quest for a good view of the stage.

Excitement scintillated in Vincent's stomach. The

cool breeze sharpened the contrast to the warmth of his skin. His mind swept away with the anticipation of the crowd. A hush fell over the spectators when the first wooden step by the stage creaked under the weight of a dancer. People craned their necks, a ripple running through the crowd at the expectation which thrummed within them all. Vincent joined in. The expectancy of the bystanders swept him with it. He rose on tip-toe, as did everyone else, just to be the first to glimpse her—to see the swish of the red skirt.

Soon enough, a murmur rose up, and another ripple spread out through the throng. Vincent caught sight of the slender woman, bright coral fabric billowing on a breath of air. She nodded towards someone behind her, out of sight. Then she stood, looked out over the crowd and raised her hand, taking up the stance of the beginning. Her other hand held the skirts up to her hip, a ruby cascade, interspersed with white and blue ribbons, falling down to her knee. A hush fell over the sunlit place. The silence was complete. Even the air stilled. Not a soul breathed in that interminable moment between her readiness and the music striking up. Everything hung in the balance.

The lull came to an end with the first, long note of the accordion. In the same instant, her heel came down with a clatter on rough wooden boards. From there, the spell of music and motion wove so tightly, it bound all those present to it. No one, not even the man leaning against the inn wall some distance away, could stay the power drawing them in. All eyes were enraptured by the performance as it unfolded before them. Gisela captivated all, and it was she who released them when the final note rang out by the downward motion of her hand, cutting the threads binding the crowd to her.

Vincent came to, snapping out of the dream-state in wonder and awe. He sucked sweet air into his burning lungs, becoming aware of the tension within that had clamped all his muscles firmly into place. With deliberate care, Vincent released each straining muscle. Where had the tension come from? His thoughts turned to something he had not noticed the previous time he watched her dance. There was a difference, or at least, something he saw now, which had been obscured before.

There was a heaviness to her movements. He thought it was the ground that held her back from the freedom of her flying leaps and effortless twirls. For it was not effortless. Chains of darkness dragged at her hands and feet, and he saw Gisela fight the obscurity of her thoughts as she launched herself into the blinding, shimmering sky of freedom and forgetfulness. *It is her escape,* he thought. Although he saw her outward appearance, as did all the other spectators, and he noted her form was pleasing to the eye, what captivated Vincent was the baring of her soul. She visualised the struggle of overcoming fears and doubts with every leap and crashed back into the depths of that inner night with every return to the earth below. Her dancing was the embodiment of the vexation he knew too well. Vincent wondered whether it was that which captivated all those people and drew them back to this place every time Gisela danced.

He pondered, too, the question of what burden a maid so young could possibly bear to manifest the human predicament so vividly. Where did the sadness he detected in her eyes come from? Why did she go directly to the church after the dancing was over? He recalled seeing her beside the effigy of the Sacred Heart when he followed her the other day. Why did she seek compassion from the gods?

Vincent watched the motion of her skirts, swishing first left, then right. It drew his attention to the sway of her hips and the curve of her buttocks, drawing his thoughts away from his questions. He found his focus returning to the woman, the elegance of her motion, the shade of her skin and the gleaming light reflecting off her obsidian hair. A longing surged in him then, more powerful than he had ever experienced before. In his mind's eye he swept back to the moment she stood before him, her gentle touch caressing the hollow at the base of his throat and the relief she brought with that contact. Feelings—and other things he did not expect—stirred within as he observed her departing figure.

"She is a special one," a gruff voice said beside him.

Vincent looked across, but when his eyes met with

only air, he found himself dropping his gaze to a short man who stood beside him. Vincent took in the large hat and nose which protruded from under the brim. The nose was unmistakable. A double-barrelled rifle hanging over the man's shoulder confirmed it was the gamekeeper. Remembering he was disguised, Vincent kept the recognition from his voice when he replied. "More than just special, surely. That young woman must be a gem among river pebbles for the gathering she draws every time she dances."

A rumbling growl emanated from the thickset man. "Be wary where you cast your eyes, *stranger*," he warned. "Gisela Winry and her family are more trouble than she's worth."

Eyebrows arching, Vincent retorted, "Surely, no harm is done with looking. Certainly not when you consider how many were looking today."

Then, Vincent spun around, hiding his irritation at the emphasis placed on "stranger" and his bafflement at the rest of the gamekeeper's warning by turning his back to the other man. Vincent strode over to where his trusted guard stood by the inn. They put their heads together, but all the while, Vincent kept an eye on the man who had been so put out by Vincent's roaming gaze. Who was the gamekeeper? What was his relationship to Gisela? And what had he meant about her family?

Once he confirmed the short gamekeeper's departure, Vincent set about finding answers to those questions, and the others that arose when Gisela finished dancing. *What better way to get answers,* Vincent thought, *than to ask the source directly?* And with that in mind, he headed to the outskirts of the village. He would contrive to meet Gisela in the lane he had scouted out earlier that afternoon, and he would satisfy his curiosity.

Vincent leaned against a tree. He chewed on a long grass stem while he waited, satisfied with the absence of traffic at that hour. It was mid-afternoon during the harvest period. Most were in their fields gathering their produce. A movement caught his eye, and his mind turned to the woman walking towards him. He watched her approach, examining the curve of her bosom beneath the tight-fitting black cardigan with a row of shiny buttons up the middle. Her waist slimmed, but was still ample compared to the women he was used to seeing. It was refreshing. Gisela's braids swung about her shoulders as she walked. He recalled the waves of her loose hair undulating about her as she danced. Now her wildness was tamed into two thick threads of black. His heart caught in his throat, though, when he saw her face. The sadness he detected during the dance bore down on her features with a vengeance. It shaded her eyes, dulling their lustre and clouding her countenance.

Vincent wanted to call out to her, to thank her for her assistance in the church, but his throat constricted around the words, cutting them off long before they could pass his lips. Then Gisela stopped as she caught sight of him standing by the tree. Her eyes widened and he noted a level of discomposure in her stance he neither expected nor understood. He saw a series of conflicting emotions flit across her face, pulling her through startled surprise, apprehension and something else he could not quite discern.

Her discomfort made him take an involuntary step forward as he cast aside the grass stem. Words tumbled from his mouth, if only to break the tension she felt. "I... I wanted to thank you. You showed me great kindness the other day, Gisela... kindness I'm not used to. I..." he trailed off, but when she didn't say anything, he rallied his courage and continued. "I see a sadness in you, which I recognise from myself. I carried a burden around in silence with me until you released it that day in the church. You opened my heart enough that I could overcome my silence while I sat in that peaceful place. Now I see you bear a similar burden, and I wish... I hope... perhaps... Perhaps I can be of some service to you, too."

He observed her hand clenching and unclenching against the fabric of her skirt. She said not a word, although he noted a struggle within her. Vincent took another step closer to her and held out his hands in a placating gesture. "You look like you don't have a friend in the world."

He wanted to say more, but when he saw a big tear roll down her cheek, he stopped. The heaviness about Gisela was palpable now. His heart constricted at the sight of her distress. In a stride, he crossed the distance between them and folded her into his arms. At first, she hesitated but then leaned in against him, and he sensed the drops coursing down her cheeks. His instinct was to comfort and hush, but then he remembered his own cathartic tears, and instead, he held her until the torrent subsided on its own.

"I'm sorry," she sniffed, stepping away from him while pressing the palms of her hands against her puffy eyes.

"There is no need to apologise," Vincent stated. "I realise it was necessary." Gisela withdrew a white, cotton square from a pocket in her skirt and continued to dab at her tear-streaked cheeks. When she didn't volunteer any information, Vincent said, "I know it can be hard to speak one's mind, especially to a total stranger, but perhaps I may provide the ears to unburden you. For I can see you have need of a friend, and I very much would like to return the favour you unwittingly bestowed upon me last time we met."

She glanced at him, her eyes still glistening. "It would not be fair of me to burden you with my troubles, sir." Her voice cracked and she dropped her gaze again, turning away from him.

"Please, call me Albert," he insisted. Then Vincent took a step in the direction she would walk to return to her father's farm. "Well, at least allow me to accompany you part of your way."

Her steps faltered, hesitant and mechanical in the beginning and then becoming smoother with every stride. He walked beside her, arms folded behind him, his hands resting in the small of his back. He remained silent. He hoped it might give Gisela the space to open up and speak. When the silence drew on, Vincent decided to switch methods.

"I spent years festering over my brother's passing," he began. "We were never close, and it happened unexpectedly. I was left bereft but could not give way to my grief because I bore the brunt of my parents' mourning. I held onto my resentment and refused to acknowledge how much I miss him, how much he actually meant to me. It all came pouring out once you left me alone the other day. Giving voice to my thoughts released me, and I don't carry that load around with me anymore. I have you to thank for this freedom."

Vincent stopped when he noted Gisela's gaze on him. Her eyes were intent, her lips pursed in contemplation. She tilted her head. "I'm sorry for your loss," she offered.

As he nodded, Vincent strode forward again. He returned to silence, observing the young woman walking beside him. She was shorter than he had expected—only a little shorter than he was. Her presence while dancing made her appear larger than life, and this realisation increased the wonder he felt in her presence. There was something different about her—something extraordinary. Nevertheless, one of her hands tugged at a braid, her eyes averted and her shoulders curved inward.

Then she spoke, haltingly at first, but her voice became smoother and fuller with each passing word until everything flowed from her in a rich alto, sleek as silk and resonant. "I had a friend. We did everything together. We had no secrets. This spring... we had a falling out. I reacted badly to something he said... but he won't let me apologise for it..."

She trailed off, her gaze fixed into the distance and silence settling between them again. She sighed, and Vincent wondered at the shadows that appeared to swirl around her. *This is only the very tip of the mountain peak*, he thought. *There is so much more bearing down on her.*

As though in answer to his unspoken thought, Gisela sucked air between her teeth, and then continued. "My father is very preoccupied with what others think, and my dancing is a sore point for him. Things seem better. He appears to have accepted it and perhaps he is proud, but I cannot help the fear gnawing at me. It is as though somewhere deep down I know this isn't going to work out. Every day I dance in the square, I glimpse something I cannot describe, but

I feel this shadow pressing down on me when the music stops. It's hard to describe. Perhaps it is a premonition... This is a fleeting moment and darkness lies at the end of the road. My father can be very hard sometimes. He is not a forgiving man, and I disobeyed him when I auditioned for the dance. He was very, very angry, and I'm not sure he's actually let it go. Like I said, he appears to have accepted... He's not vindictive, but I can't shake that he is not happy with me—that he'll make me pay."

Vincent observed her incisors biting down on her lower lip, forcefully closing the floodgates. Her arms folded over her chest, and she hugged herself for a moment before she gave a little laugh. "Sometimes I say the silliest things." Gisela brushed a hand over her brow, wiping the grey clouds from her face. She shook her head and smiled, a radiant beam of sunshine. "I do believe the dragons make things work out in the end. Everything is as they intend. I struggle with it sometimes, but I know this is the truth."

Time paused. Vincent leaned forward, a torrent of emotions sizzling through him. He wished to embrace her, to touch his lips to hers. Her cocoa gaze drew him in. Vincent felt the whirlpool tugging at him. Desire. Longing. Hope. Gisela's eyes flitted over his lips and then returned to meet his own. He pulled back, exercising all of his self-control to refuse the primal response of his body. His mind forced its way through the tumultuous haze. *Make a move too soon, and you'll ruin any chance you have. Calm down!*

He straightened, touching her shoulder as much to steady himself as to reassure her. "Thank you for sharing your thoughts with me. I am honoured you deem me worthy. You are probably right about the dragon lords. If life were easy, we would never achieve anything. It is through our struggles with our difficulties that we grow." He paused. Her eyes shone. "I also know you are in haste to return to your family, so I shall not keep you any longer," he said, moving away. He took a step in the direction they had come. Then he paused again, and glanced at her. "I... I sincerely wish you might allow me to... to accompany you again," he faltered.

Her face creased into a warm smile, her eyes glowing to match the autumn afternoon. "I would like that very much, Albert," she said, her voice husky.

19

Gisela spent several days floating on a cloud, part confusion and part contentment. Although she revelled in the new-found buoyancy, there was still a tendency for her thoughts to turn downward, much as each cloud has the capacity for rain even as it wings its way through the skies. Gisela pondered the man, Albert, and the sincerity she detected in his confession: his resentment of his dead brother. The thought of his tragic loss, brought her compassion simmering to the surface. She also contemplated the levity of her own problems in comparison. Clearly, her fears and the loss of Hilarion's friendship were nothing compared to the grief of losing a brother, whether beloved or not.

While she picked grapes from first light until darkness blanketed the valley, Gisela mulled over her promise to walk with Albert again after her next practise session. She struggled to understand why she had agreed to such a thing, knowing full well the exposure it could lead to—and the consequences. On more than one occasion, the memory of her father's rage from that evening in the spring, plagued her, dampening her trembling palms with anxiety.

Notwithstanding, Gisela spent more hours recalling the moment the young man she knew as Albert leaned towards her as though wishing to give into the physical attraction they seemed to share. Yet, he had withdrawn before allowing their bodies to rule their actions. In her mind's eye, she relived the intensity of his amber gaze attesting to the effort it took him to draw away. Gisela's heart glowed with admiration for the restraint he showed in that moment. While she thought about the incident, she became aware of a shift in her attitude towards him. She trusted Albert. At some deep, inexplicable level. Her trust was clear as a high-mountain lake. Gisela also realised she trusted Albert more than she ever had Hilarion.

Reason leapt up, showering her with disdain. *Trust? A stranger? After Hilarion?* She knew it was madness—stupidity even—but, still, Gisela was certain she could depend upon Albert. It was a visceral knowing, deep and immovable as the bedrock beneath the mountains. She could not tell how she knew, but she did. Every now and then she allowed the conviction of her intuition to swat at the reservations her rational brain tossed about with pompous authority. Albert was trustworthy. Less than an hour later, she was back in the throes of doubt, battling the hydra of her good sense, repeating the ordeal again, and again.

By the time she caught sight of Albert, leaning against the tree in the same place Hilarion had stood, so many months before, anxiety and uncertainty twisted her intestines into knots. He smiled at her, blowing away the tension. It was a light autumn breeze dancing away the dry brown leaves of her worries. Her lips twitched heavenward in a spontaneous reply.

"You were inspirational as ever today, Gisela. It is a gift to see you dance." His voice was constricted with emotion. She wondered what else he wanted to say but struggled to put into words.

"Thank you," she murmured, eyes boring into her dirty boots while she tried to curb the flaming heat searing through her neck and cheeks. Gisela's attention was drawn back to him when he moved. His spotless boots crunched on the gravel of the road when he stepped out onto it. In relief, she turned away from her discomfort and stepped up beside him.

Out of the corner of her eye, she took note of her companion. Albert was a little taller than she was, his face framed with thick, straight hair. He folded his arms behind his back as he walked, so different from the stance of the men she knew. He wore a simple brown shirt and breeches, and Gisela detected that they were very clean and quite new. There was also a softness to him, which she found intriguing. He was unlike any of the hard-working, tough men she knew from her home and acquaintances. She could not place what it was that made him stand out as different, but she detected that some quality did exist. The contrast sparked her curiosity, but she also didn't want to seem rude. Her jaw clenched, snapping shut the sluice and forcing back a flood of impolite questions.

While she struggled with herself, Gisela glanced back at Albert, who kept silent. Her head tilted involuntarily when she became aware of the humour glinting in his eyes. There was also kindness in his face, and she realised she could let her guard down a little, for he was not like other men she knew. He reinforced this thought by asking a question she did not expect.

"When do you plan to dance again after the harvest festival ends?"

She jerked her head up. Her heart started thumping faster while she blinked. She looked at him blankly for a moment and then answered in an indistinct murmur, "I don't know." She paused, coming to grips with her confusion and at long last admitted, "I hadn't actually thought about it."

He stopped short, and stared at her. She noted the way his eyebrows arched into the centre of his forehead. "The best dancer ever seen in all of Vendale, *hasn't thought about it*?"

Ears heating in response to his incredulity, Gisela squirmed on the spot for a moment to gather her thoughts. "I... I only wanted to do this. My dream has always been dancing at the harvest festival. Just getting to this point has been hard enough. You have no idea how awful it was to get my father to even allow this. Being Harvest Queen is an honour, and I'm overwhelmed by it all. And I'm hardly the best dancer in all of Vendale."

She paused to swallow, and he took the opportunity to emphasise, "You weren't chosen for nothing. You are an incredible dancer. It is not just an honour but something you deserve. The other girls pale in comparison."

Gisela shrugged. "I never had any aspiration for it. I just love to dance, and I wanted to be in the harvest festival. What happens afterwards is not really important. I'll marry whomever my father chooses for me, and then I'll have a family to raise. Old Mrs Smith mentioned I could join her and eventually take over as instructor—"

A strangled sound, somewhere between a cry and a groan, escaped Albert. She glanced at him, and seeing the disbelief in his eyes, she shifted. Her hand grasped a braid. While she tugged on her hair in apprehension, Gisela's thoughts behaved like crickets, hopping about erratically. *Why shouldn't I settle down? Everyone does that, right? Could I dance? Father would never allow it. And do I even want to? Would a husband father chooses for me allow it? It's so overwhelming. I don't feel ready for this.*

Having collected his thoughts, he reached out and

grasped her shoulder. Her gaze snapped up to meet his, and she heard the increased tempo of her heart. The intensity reflected in his eyes brought his voice to a lower pitch when he said, "Gisela, you are the most amazing dancer I have ever seen. No one has your talent. It would be easy for you to become the lead dancer at court."

She laughed. It was so absurd. *Court? Impossible.* She shook her head, but his eyes blazed molten amber in response. "You would throw away your gift? You belittle yourself and deprive the world of upliftment. Why do you think they come to watch you every practise?"

She shook her head again. "They're just coming to watch the practise. It's nice to watch. I used to do it every year."

A big sigh poured out of him then, and his arm fell to his side. "You don't see it. You are oblivious to your own talent..."

His shoulders slumped as he shook his head, muttering under his breath at how blind she was. Gisela saw the flame in him sputter. Helplessness engulfed him when he murmured, "A world without you dancing in it isn't worth living in."

It was Gisela's turn to reach out to him. Her hand hovered just above his shoulder, almost touching. A wave of feelings coursed through her. The realist was the first to sort its way through the mire. "What do you want me to do? My father says dancing is a sinful thing and only brings dishonour. I already crossed him by auditioning for the harvest festival, and becoming Harvest Queen forced his hand. He would rather die than let me dance for a living. It would be shameful, and I could not do that to him. I never had any intention of becoming a dancer. I didn't even mean to be picked at the audition. I just wanted to dance before an audience that one time."

Her raised hand slumped to her side. The other still clasped her braid. She turned and started walking again, trying to distance herself from the disappointment and incredulity streaming from Albert. *It's unrealistic and dangerous,* she thought. *He cannot understand how it is with father. He could—*

Her thought was roughly cut off when she was spun around, the force of the motion pitching her forward. She collided with Albert, who held her shoulders in a firm, unwavering grasp. "But what if this is a gift from the gods?" His voice was strained, harsher than usual. "You were clearly born to dance, Gisela. That is a gift. If you don't dance, what will become of you? What will happen to you if dancing were suddenly torn from you, and you were left with nothing more than your memories of those moments? Could you live like that? A shadow of yourself?"

Gisela swallowed. Her heart was misbehaving, skittering like a shy animal with no rhythm to speak of. In detachment, she felt mist filling her mind. Thinking became difficult. She struggled to even hear what he said to her. His fingers dug into her shoulders, but the discomfort was nothing like the pain constricting her breath. Heat she could not define blossomed within her, and her breath hitched in her chest. He was too close. His eyes trapped her and, what with the erratic beating of her heart, she felt like a songbird flapping to be free of a cage. Her attention was drawn to his lips. He was breathing hard, and he had stopped talking.

She noted a flicker in his gaze, as though he hesitated, pondering an unspoken thought. Then, he pulled her forward, locking his lips onto hers. The contact sent flashes of lightning coursing through her body. Gisela gasped and pulled back, but the intensity of the heat flowing through her overrode her rational mind and social training. Her body leaned in again, despite everything. She accepted this second kiss, which was softer and more sensual than the first. Sparkles lit up her frame, effervescent bubbles seethed inside her while his hand slipped up to the base of her skull, and his tongue explored hers.

After an eternity in a heartbeat, they drew apart. Gisela swallowed and lowered her gaze to avoid contact. A dense fog permeated her mind, making thought impossible. She became aware of her fingers brushing over her lips. It was an instinctive motion, and it grounded her. It stilled the reeling from the tumultuous momentum of passion that had ripped her into a cyclone of emotion and unfamiliar sensations.

Next, her awareness settled on Albert, who was

breathing hard. Her eyes flickered to his, and she noted they had softened to honey. He leaned forward and murmured in her ear, "It makes me angry that you would disregard something so meaningful. Your dancing brings joy and life to dreary lives. Please... just think about it. Consider what you would be doing for others—and yourself. You matter. I would hate to see you lose the magic spark you have when you dance. That would be a tragedy."

Gisela swallowed again. Her mind still laboured in the swamp, unable to find its way through the fog. She looked at him without saying a word and felt like an idiot because she struggled to get her thoughts to function. Still, Albert didn't seem bothered by it. The tenderness he bestowed on her was another blow to her already reeling brain. It just washed over her, but his words were an arrow—sharp and fast and accurate.

"I cannot bear to think of you trapped in a cage, least of all, one of your own making."

By this time, Albert had taken her hand up in his. The warmth of his touch sent a shiver to her elbow, but in the miasma of her befuddlement, Gisela hardly noticed. Albert raised her hand and gently brushed his lips over her knuckles. The contact was so soft, and yet, it was more sensuous than all that had gone before—the reverberating knell of a gong in her corporeal temple.

He stepped back. From the distance of her hazy dream, Gisela observed the strength of his will. She saw, clear as mountain air, that he wished for nothing more than to fold her into his arms and continue their embrace. He took another deliberate, torturous step. With the stretch between them growing, Gisela came to her senses. Her eyes thanked him for his forbearance and she stepped away, in the direction of her father's farm. She took two more faltering steps and then turned.

Albert was watching her. She met his gaze, and her voice surprised her with unanticipated steadiness. "Can I see you tomorrow?" She received a radiant smile in reply. She shocked herself with her own forwardness. Thoughts fell over each other to get her attention, but she focused on the only one that mattered to her in that precise moment. "I have to help with the last of the harvest in the morning, but I can get away in the afternoon."

"I can meet you after the hunt," he said. "I shall ride with my lord into the forest at daybreak."

"Can you meet me in the forest behind my house two hours before sunset?"

Eyes gleaming, he nodded. "Absolutely!" he called out, joy buoying his tone. Gisela flashed a bright smile before whipping around and hastening home.

20

Autumn in the valley came with a decisive swoop. It took one stroke of the artist's brush to turn forest green to amber. Early morning was marked with a chill, foreshadowing the coming winter, and mist—the great muffler of the vale—which blanketed fields and forests. Few were about in the dimness before sunrise, but one figure did startle roosting birds.

Hilarion whistled a tune, his eyes bright in anticipation of this day. The unexpected sound startled other creatures, too. He smiled, belying the rumours claiming his lips were unyielding rock. The jaunty sound accompanied his light pace, almost a skip, but which would have been classified as a shuffle by the discerning onlooker. As things were, though, the only beholders of Hilarion's prancing steps were the swallows startled by his passing, a family of quail huddling at the base of a bush he passed by, and a fox who pricked its russet ears at the commotion.

Reaching a lane, Hilarion restrained his overt cheeriness. He marched towards the village of Ylvaton in comparative silence. The crunch of his boots on gravel was the only sound to accompany his passing. The mist began its futile battle against the sun's bright spears. Each new ray thrust the grey haze further into retreat, and it was not long before only smoky tendrils remained, disintegrating before the onslaught of light and heat.

When he reached the outskirts of the village, Hilarion noted the sounds accompanying the inhabitants' waking: the soft murmur of talking, clanging of pots, sizzling food, wails from uncooperative children. The village coming alive upon arrival of the solar disk was a scene Hilarion did not witness often. His breath slowed, his body relaxing even more as he absorbed the details of human life around him. His eyes widened, and his lips twitched with the awareness of wakefulness among people in contrast to the animal kingdom he called home.

He rounded the corner of the mayor's house and was met with the sight of about ten horses milling about. Some were riderless, led two at a time by stable hands. Others already bowed their necks under pressure from reins. An even greater number of people were on foot, rifles slung over their backs, shouting above the din of hooves and keeping their distance from them. Hilarion approached the group as a scuffle broke out where one of the mounts jerked its hind-legs in response to another steed nearby. The innocent victim responded with flattened ears and bared teeth while stomping on the ground with a thud. Some invectives later, comparative calm was once again restored.

Moments passed, and a hush fell over the party. A tall man, dressed in subdued colours strode forward. His coat was grey, and, yet, the skill of the weaving left it shimmering in the early morning sun. He wore knee-high boots of finest leather and a grey hat with broad gold trimming. Hilarion felt his breath catch in his throat at his first glimpse of a lord suited up for the hunt. The man swung into the saddle with a practised motion and whirled his horse towards Hilarion.

"Well met, gamekeeper!" he exclaimed as an orderly column of men and horses materialised behind him. "It promises to be a fine day for the hunt."

Hilarion nodded in answer. Reconsidering his silence, he added, "There was much activity within the woods an hour ago. It is an excellent occasion, and you are certain to have your sport."

A smirk creased the cheeks on the lord's visage. He gestured with a gloved hand and Hilarion led the way, keeping his pace brisk in his awareness of the impatience many in the group showed. He trusted that he didn't slow down the hunting party's progress too much and hoped all would go well, so he might celebrate this day.

The sun stood high in the blue canopy. It radiated heat onto the golden forest, light absorbed and transformed into burnished leaves. A horn sounded through the trees, the sharp call bouncing through the air, alerting everyone in fields and on farms that prey was in sight. The proclamation still reverberated from the woods when the ground trembled with onrushing hoof-beats.

Hilarion jogged along at a steady pace, keeping an eye on the flocks of birds fluttering up in fright and returning to their perches in an undulating wave. He kept pace with five others on foot. He glanced behind and noticed another three falling back, unable to keep the relentless pace set by the horsemen interested only in the chase. His mind wandered to the moment when they picked out a russet coat slinking through the underbrush, and the excitement that rippled through the hunting party. Then, the horn-blower had emitted his deafening blast, freezing the fox for an interminable moment before it took self-preservation to heart and fled—a rust-red streak against the impressionistic flecks of green, brown and yellow. Hilarion's heart had leapt at the ensuing thunderous vibration and accompanying shouts, which grew distant in a short time. From there, his musings hovered in a daydream about the praise and recommendation he would receive.

Returning to the present, Hilarion noticed the forest's stillness. Only the leaves sighed in a rustling symphony as the breeze sped by. There were no flocks hovering in the air above the trees, screeching their disgruntlement at the commotion below. The silence was even more profound because of the din preceding it. It gnawed at Hilarion's innards, as though the natural state of the forest were in some way aberrant.

He increased his pace, and soon he left the other men behind. He hastened to the area where last the birds had taken to the skies. He also kept an eye on the tell-tale signs of hoof-prints and the passage of ten horses through the dense wood. Chest heaving, a stabbing pain rending his left side, Hilarion rounded a bend in the path and stopped. His heart jumped into his mouth, then fluttered back into his ribcage. Eyes popping, Hilarion choked down what felt like a mixture of sandpaper and bile, while his stomach clenched into a solid rock, immovable and unreceptive.

The company of horsemen stood, transfixed in a recently harvested wheat field. Calf-high stalks stuck out in rows above the dark soil. Tension radiated off the whole company like the arm of an archer drawing his bow to hold, waiting for the perfect moment to let fly. Hilarion made out the young lord at the front of the group, relaxed and in conversation with Gisela, who stood, arms flung wide in a commanding gesture to block their path. Her dark eyes flashed, and her grey skirts danced about her legs in the gentle air. Behind her rose a tall hedge, but Hilarion's attention was drawn to Gisela and her noticeable disregard for the aristocrat's superior station.

Pushing forward, Hilarion rounded the company, coming close enough to hear what passed between Gisela and the man atop his horse. Hilarion also noticed the intensity of the aristocrat's gaze as he sat in his saddle, appraising the young woman barring his path.

"...is private property. It is hardly my fault the fox ran under the hedge, into the last vineyard that hasn't yet been harvested. You cannot expect His Highness, the king, to accept a mere fox as cause for the destruction of his finest wine?" Gisela's voice was sharp, stinging like acid.

The young lord astride his grey charger held Gisela's steadfast gaze and replied, his lips twitching, "No, we could not allow that. Finest wine, you say? What estate is this?"

"Wyndemere," she said, lifting her chin as her back straightened with pride.

The horseman's eyes widened a hair's breadth, and then he wheeled his horse, calling over his shoulder, his voice indifferent, "apologies for the fright, Miss. Since we have lost the purpose of our sport here, we shall be on our way." He signalled the others with a flick of the reins, and the horses pranced back onto the forest path. Gisela turned to go, but stopped when Hilarion stormed up to her.

"What do you think you are doing?" he exclaimed, beside himself.

Gisela's eyebrows flew almost to her hairline. "Protecting my father's crops. What do you think?" Her voice was even more asinine than it had been when she addressed the lord moments before.

"The harvest is over. Everyone knows that. Word was brought in yesterday, and the festival is set for tomorrow. There are no more grapes to harvest. What are you on about?"

"You think it's all right for his almightiness to destroy our livelihood just because the fruit is in? What about the vines? My father's grandfather planted these, and I will not see them trampled by some lordling and his underlings in pursuit of a hapless fox. And you, of all people, Hilarion, should understand how important this vineyard is to my family. There are droves of worthy game in the woods, just over there. Why are you so hung up about a single fox?"

It was Hilarion's turn to frown. "It is the sport that matters. The thrill of the chase, not so much the creature. I don't expect you to understand. You have gotten yourself into frightful trouble which could have repercussions on your family. This man is not some little lordling. He is clearly important. You haven't been around his retainers."

Hilarion drew breath, and Gisela took the opportunity to respond. "That still doesn't give him the right to destroy a functioning vineyard for the sport of chasing a fox. Clearly, he agreed with me, because I don't see him kicking up a fuss about it. So, run along and find him something else to chase. I have better things to do than to do your work for you. Why didn't you tell him there were vineyards in this area, on the outskirts of the forest? He would surely have avoided coming here and saved me the madness of rushing over in time to stop them from charging over the hedge. If you did your job properly, the rest of us could focus on ours."

Then she spun around and marched off without a backward glance. Hilarion growled out a string of oaths and trudged back into the trees, hoping they would soon find something else to assuage the lord and his hunting party. While he walked, Hilarion kept returning to the scene on the Winry farm. Something about the young lord's gaze niggled at the back of Hilarion's mind. He ground his teeth as he thought and thought about what his intuition was trying to tell him.

For most of the afternoon, he mulled over the incident, his beagle-brain too stubborn to let go of this fox-thought, no matter how it tried to elude him. While the hunting party spent fruitless hours and eventually gave up when the air turned chill with steel-grey clouds amassing on the horizon, Hilarion still worried at what he knew was a significant moment. What was it about the lord's gaze that bothered him?

It was only when he returned to his impoverished home and set aside his deliberation to consider the following day's start to the harvest festival, that everything fell into place. His thoughts of the festivities and Gisela's role as Harvest Queen on the second night brought the flashing lightning strike of insight. Gisela dancing. The stranger ogling her during her practise session. The look in the lord's eyes as he appraised Gisela. The immensity of the shuddering realisation left Hilarion gasping. Could it be? Was it possible? Or was he entirely mistaken?

Coming to his feet, he tore along the forest path he'd avoided whenever possible since the spring. If the suspicion his stomach and heart confirmed were true, then Gisela had to be warned. She could be in very real trouble—danger even—and he had to do something about it. Hurtling as fast as his legs would go, Hilarion had no care for the twigs that snapped across his face. He barely felt the stinging sensations that cut across his cheeks every now and then.

He came to the edge of the tree line and headed to the Winry farmhouse. There was no sign of Gisela. Mrs Winry sat rocking and crocheting beside the door. Her face brightened when she looked up and met his worried gaze.

"Hilarion," she said, her tone conveying delight. "It is wonderful to see you. How have you been?"

He nodded, dropping his gaze to the toe of his boot. "Uh... fine. Mrs Winry." He squirmed with one foot and then added, as an afterthought, "And you?"

"Oh, we've been very well. The harvest is in, and we've had quite a good year, despite the losses from that unexpected rain a few weeks ago. All's well and ready for the festival tomorrow. We'll be sending the last of the barrels to the storage in Ylvaton tomorrow morning. We have missed you so. It is lovely to see you well and thriving. I heard you found some huntsmen. I'm truly glad for you..."

Hilarion allowed her words to wash over him. It was a trained habit for him to phase out at some point in Mrs Winry's incessant monologues. He could not remember a time she had not poured forth words as soon as he was nearby. He wondered whether she was always like this, or whether it had something to do with him and her friendship with his mother.

Pulling himself back from the stupor Mrs Winry's words lulled him into, Hilarion blinked, took a deep breath and asked, "Where is Gisela?"

The dumpy woman, her hands turning yarn into something beautiful with dexterity, paused her flow of words to look up at Hilarion. "She said she was going for a walk now that the harvest is over. She mentioned she would probably be late because she wanted to walk out all the aches and pains from the work these past weeks. She laboured ever so diligently all these months. For once, she really did everything expected of her. Allowing her to dance has had so many wonderful benefits. She's been absolutely charming."

Hilarion nodded, gave an awkward bow, made his excuses and returned the way he had come.

21

Vincent wheeled his horse. Relief soothed the rushing hum of his blood into a gentle ripple. The pleasant autumn air filled his lungs, stilling the frantic whirlwind of his thoughts. *Thank the dragons I didn't give myself away.* His hand relaxed on the pommel of his sword, revealing the carved bone stag with majestic antlers on the hilt. *No one seemed to notice the sword either*, he sighed.

Knowing Gisela only saw a rude lord, with no consideration for anything other than his own sport, eased his tension, and Vincent noticed his horse pricking its ears and lengthening its stride in response to that release. His entourage clustered around him, talking excitedly. He heard some call for the young woman to answer for her rudeness, while others focused their attention back to the hunt, voicing their hope for more sport.

Giving the second group their desire, Vincent called out, "Who will find me a less slippery fox?" His heart did not resonate with the laugh he forced out. As soon as he was certain the others would leave him alone, Vincent diverted all thoughts from the hunt or anything other than Gisela. He even allowed his horse freedom to choose its path, granting it authority over its own hooves and trusting in the power of herd-mentality to ensure he stayed with his people. With the tension and his mind freed up, Vincent allowed his heart free rein.

Gisela. He remembered her standing before him, hands outstretched. She was fierce in her protection of the things she loved. She did dangerous things to do what she deemed just. Vincent's heart clenched as his mind reconstructed the moment she hurtled between his galloping horse and the furry, russet streak which, moments later, slipped under the hedge.

"What are you doing?" his memory replayed his own terrified cry of horror which, in hindsight, he hoped she interpreted as arrogant irritation. He remembered catching himself and compelling himself to add, *"Get out of the way!"*

She had not. Gisela stood firm, her resolve rippling through the air around her. "I will not," she stated, an unmoving mountain reverberating in her voice. "This is not the forest. You have no right to hunt here. This is private land—and cultivated. Turn back," she added, a waver in her voice.

Despite every fiber wishing to heed her command, Vincent instead retaliated, "The fox left the forest. It is there," and he pointed behind her.

Gisela did not flinch. "The fox does not know the laws of the king." He remembered how she paused, adding the weight of silence to the thought, *but you do,* before she said, "This is private property. It is hardly my fault the fox ran under the hedge, into the last vineyard that hasn't yet been harvested. You cannot expect His Highness, the king, to accept a mere fox as cause for the destruction of his finest wine?"

Forcing his mind back onto his surroundings, he noted his men were still searching fruitlessly. Sighing, Vincent returned to his memory of the woman who sent his head spinning with her blazing determination and the breeze playing with her skirts. He knew it cost him something, not giving in to his first impulse to spring to her side and pull her into his embrace. More than anything, he wanted to assure her she was safe and promise he would keep her that way. *I had to keep up the ruse*, he justified to himself. *I had to.* Then self-doubt and uncertainty, two companions he knew well, began their relentless assault, but on this occasion, he felt their stinging remarks were justified.

For once in his life, Vincent found himself in the unusual circumstance where his desires and his thoughts aligned. He should have given up the ruse. He should have come clean with her. *I should tell her,* he thought. *When I see her later, I must tell her the truth.*

In response, his rational mind clamped down, consolidating its message with fear, *It is impossible. Everything will be lost with that action. She'll grow further away. No, she'll turn away. I cannot tell her who I am. I must not. I must keep this secret a little longer, or I'll lose her entirely.*

At long last, after hours of torment and no resolution, Vincent called off the hunt and rode back to the inn. He hoped his retinue would ascribe the cloak of despondence wrapped around his figure to his thoughts on the disappointing hunt. Vincent knew only one of his followers was aware of how much he hated hunting, but Oskar said nothing. Vincent was grateful his friend held his silence at that moment. He longed for a moment to speak with Madeleine, for she would know what to do.

A short while later, Vincent, now dressed in the brown garb of Albert, slipped out of the inn unnoticed and accompanied only by his stoic second shadow. Together they headed back into the forest behind the Winry family's vineyard. While the bodyguard slipped out of sight, Vincent sat down on a rock, leaning on a tree trunk, awaiting the hour appointed by Gisela.

He pushed aside his ponderous thoughts from earlier in the day and instead focused on the building excitement clenching in his stomach at the thought he would spend time alone with this woman. All he wanted was to be close to her, to hear her melodious voice speaking in confidence—to him, and him alone. He stared over at the farmhouse where it gleamed in the sun. *A warm and homely place*, he thought. It brought him comfort, something his own home never had. Vincent imagined what kind of life Gisela might lead there. *Beloved daughter. Comfortable. But with hard work,* he had to remind himself. Tending a vineyard was no easy thing, and there were also fields like the one that separated him from her at that moment. Fields that needed to be tilled and tended.

Recalling the fierceness blazing in her eyes earlier that day, Vincent realised she was also proud of the work she did. He smiled. He could understand that. His one brief day working for an honest wage in the warehouse in Port Averly had shown him the satisfaction that comes with work. Doing something and seeing the result filled a person with meaning. *Nevertheless, she's been saddened by things. This farmstead is not as peaceful as I believe.* His thoughts drifted to her words about her father. He conjured up a proud, unyielding man, quick to anger and a little brutish. Rippling muscles and sun-darkened, leathery skin. Plate-sized hands, rough and calloused from years of tending vines.

Then his thoughts dissipated when he caught sight of the figure crossing the open space behind the house. She wore the same grey dress, but had slung a bright green shawl over her shoulders. Her braids swung about her shoulders and her face beamed at him when she was close enough to see him. Staying in the tree-line, out of sight from the farmhouse, Vincent rose to greet her.

"Well met, oh radiant defender of foxes."

She broke his gaze, smiling with embarrassment and kept walking. He joined her and noted a hint of pleasure when she glanced up, her lips still twitching. She said, "So you were there. I didn't see you." When he didn't say anything, she asked, "Did you find another creature for your lord to torment?"

Vincent smiled in response to her wicked tone. "Alas, no. The foxes and deer learned their lesson for today."

They walked together in silence for a time, side by side, enjoying the cool shade beneath the trees and the whirlwind of leaves dancing around them. Vincent glanced about, but could not see his bodyguard. *Silent and discreet as ever*, he thought. He turned his full attention back to Gisela. She appeared quite comfortable beside him, but he also had the impression she had a destination in mind. He could tell they weren't ambling aimlessly.

"Are we going anywhere special?" he asked. Gisela fidgeted with her braid. She opened her mouth to speak, then stopped. After a moment, it shut again. He chuckled. "Lead away, my lady. No need to give it away. I would follow you to the edge of Vendale without question."

Now you've done it, he thought reproachfully as he watched her discomfort increase. She tugged at her braid with force and studied the ground ahead of her trudging feet. Vincent resisted the temptation to reach out and loosen the fingers yanking at her hair. Instead, he changed the subject, "I heard the festival starts tomorrow."

Her face lit up, and she relaxed. "Yes. At sundown tomorrow the festivities begin. Four days long. It is our favourite festival. People come from all over the valley to taste the wine from previous harvests which we bottled a few months ago. I can't wait for the cream buns and—" She broke off. Disappointment flitted across her face. "I forgot," she murmured. "Father said I may only attend on the days I'll be dancing. I will only be going the day after tomorrow and on the last day." She shook her head, scattering the sadness off her in an arc.

"Well, no matter," she said, taking a lighter step forward. Then, as if on an impulse, she grabbed his hand. "Come. One of my favourite places is just around the next bend."

She led the way and Vincent followed, trying all the while to still his heart, which trembled in response to her firm, warm grasp on his fingers. They rounded a rocky outcrop and Gisela stepped off the path, her boots crackling over fallen leaves and twigs. She let his hand fall so she could steady herself as she climbed over a tricky patch of rocks and roots. Vincent held back a sigh while his hand tingled in the sudden coolness her warmth left behind. He didn't have long to lament the loss of physical contact.

Moments later, Gisela pulled aside a branch, revealing a cosy hollow, walled off by moss-covered boulders on one side and a thicket of shrubs. The leafy branch concealed it well enough. Bending over, she ducked under the branch and stepped inside.

Vincent stopped short, his mind invaded by the curve of her buttocks. With a force of will he didn't know he possessed, he resisted the temptation to stretch out and run his hand over her striking contours. Only his fingers twitched. Then the leaves swung back into their usual place and cut off his view. He breathed in several slow, deep breaths trying to calm his palpitating heart and the yearning that was taking over his rationality. *Get a grip*, he thought.

The leaves rustled again as they were pushed outward. Gisela's large eyes peered out from her oval face. Her head tilted to one side questioningly. Then she beckoned. Vincent followed even as a turmoil of mixed emotions whisked through him. *Almighty dragons! I hope I know what I'm doing,* he thought as the branch snapped back into place behind him, leaves rustling and then falling silent.

22

Gisela's heart pounded in the back of her throat. He was so close to her. The intensity of his amber eyes brought an instinctive reaction. She scooted further into the hollow, dropped her gaze and avoided contact. She noticed a yellow leaf clinging to her skirt. Thankful for the distraction, she picked it up, studying it as though she'd never seen such a thing before. She dared glance over at Albert, but winced at the painful constriction her heart produced. *Why did I never have this kind of reaction with Hilarion? What does this man have that Hilarion doesn't? I came here with Hilarion all the time, and it never made any difference, but with Albert it's... Why does my heart stutter so?*

She sat in silence, focusing on the pace of her breathing, trying to slow it. She twisted the leaf between her fingers, dropping it and turning her attention to the canopy rustling above them in a golden dance while she tugged at one of her braids. The man beside her maintained the little distance between them. He, too, remained silent, but when Gisela glanced over at him, she saw he was studying her. Their gazes locked and no matter how much she wished to break the contact, she could not.

He raised a hand, caressing her cheek with a gentle movement. His touch sent a shiver through Gisela, but she leaned forward. He dropped his hand as he murmured, "I never knew I could feel this way. When I'm with you, everything is brighter, bolder. I feel hot and cold at the same time. I'd never imagined this many emotions could find a way to exert themselves simultaneously. At times, I feel I must be mad, but then I realise that it's just because I've never felt this way before. I've never been in love before. I had no idea. And it just came, out of the blue, like a lightning strike. Sudden and without looking for it or even knowing what was happening. I just fell... in love..."

His voice trailed off, and Gisela saw his eyes waver. The tumult of thoughts she saw spilling through those windows to his soul stilled her own confusion. *We are the same*, she thought. *Neither of us knows where this will take us, but it is happening as we speak, and we cannot fight it.* He opened his mouth as if to continue, but Gisela shifted. She leaned towards him, brushing her fingertips across his lips. Almost imperceptibly, she shook her head. She tried to speak, but no sound could cross the barrier her hammering heart created at the back of her throat.

"Oh, Gisela," he whispered and pulled her to him.

Their lips touched. Although it was uncoordinated and clumsy, the kiss sent shooting stars through her body. If she thought the sensations from the day before were wonderful, now the fireworks that set off in her stomach only fanned a deeper flame. Her body took over while her mind hung back in a nebulous haze. Gisela leaned onto him, her hands pressed against his chest, her mouth locked to his. She shifted again to change the uncomfortable angle, and she straddled him. His lips became more insistent while his arms circled her. His hands explored her back, tugging the shawl so it fell away.

Gisela felt his body respond to hers, and she gasped at the hardness straining against the fabric of his breeches. Heat bloomed from the place on her inner thigh where it pressed against her. Flames ignited in the deep place within her, a dark secret place she'd never really been aware of, coming unexpectedly to light with an overpowering urgency. His teeth grazed over her lower lip, eliciting a gasp from her and then his tongue searched for, and found, the tip of hers. More shuddering sensations rippled through her as she responded.

Turning her head, she inhaled. Never breaking his stride, his lips traversed her jaw and wandered over her neck to her collarbone. Gisela felt her back arch, pressing her body against his, and she felt the burning heat of his erection shift against the deep place between her legs. Her urgency increased. With trembling fingers, she fumbled with the buttons of his shirt. She needed to feel his skin. The overpowering desire to press her hands against his warm chest, skin on skin, consumed all other thoughts.

His lips found hers again, and she lost herself in the softening hardness of his devouring kisses. Their tongues danced in time to the complex rhythm of her unevenly palpitating heart, which raced on in the clickety-clack of a multiple shuffle, wing-and-clip combo. Gisela hardly felt his fingers fumbling over the row of buttons at the front of her bodice. She did notice when her breasts spilled free, the coolness of the air reinforcing the sense of freedom.

She gasped, her back arching while her hips pushed further against him of their own volition. The embrace of their lips ended, she breathed calming gulps of air, cooling the conflagration within her, but to no avail. His incendiary lips continued their dance on her throat and exposed shoulder while a hand cupped and caressed one of her exposed breasts. A moan escaped her while her nipples became sentinels, standing to attention before their lord.

Then his tongue found a nipple. Gisela had never imagined the intensity of such sensations. Wondrous ecstasy coursed through her. One of his hands, warm—almost burning—pressed into the small of her back, while the other found her knee, rising above it to where her stocking ended. His naked touch on her leg sent tingles seething through her blood. He drew her mouth back to his and paused with his hand on her thigh, his touch so close to that part of her yearning for release and, yet, not granting it. Her own hands began caressing his chest frantically. She explored the soft downy hair on his torso, the curve of his muscles—soft but defined. His skin seemed to blaze at the contact of her fingers and his own hand responded, drifting onto the soft mound of her sex.

Gisela did not notice his teeth becoming more insistent, grazing her lower lip. Her attention was completely captured by the pleasure his fingers called forth as he explored her. She broke free from his kisses, her lungs aching for air while he stroked her, his fingers circling. His mouth was on her other breast then—tugging, teasing. Then his soft caress of her sanctuary paused. She quivered, suspended above him. Her whole body tensed with her desire for his next touch. It came with a decisive plunge. Gisela cried out as his finger dove into her, sending a lightning strike from elbows to fingertips. She gasped in the pause as he withdrew his hand, but then her body strained again, begging for more, and he granted it. When he next withdrew, his thumb flicked over the hardened button, and her own body responded, pressing her damp tunnel over his outstretched finger.

His shuddering groan brought her attention back

from the ecstasy of her own pleasure. She became aware of the intensity of his desire that blazed in his eyes. He withdrew his hand from beneath her skirts and pulled her against him. He held her for what seemed an eternity before he croaked, his voice harsh, "I cannot hold back, if... if we go on."

Gisela swallowed, but she knew there was no turning back now. Not with the conflagration inside her, nor with the dampness within her that longed for more than just a finger. Longed for and demanded. Words came then, decisive and unwavering. "I don't want you to hold back, Albert."

His eyes flicked away from her for a moment. Then they were back, drawing her into their deep, gravitational pull. She hung in the balance, unable and not interested in breaking his gaze. She felt safe with him —despite her utter vulnerability. Love stretched out wings, and she soared into the heavens of his unwavering scrutiny. Then, he lifted her, and placed her on her back, stretching out beside her. He stroked her cheek as he planted a kiss on her forehead. She shifted against the hardness of the earth beneath her, finding a more comfortable angle. He toyed with the end of her braid, pulling the ribbon in slow motion until it unravelled. While his fingers teased out the strands of her ebony tresses, he murmured, "I never imagined I could feel this way." His finger glided over the shining, obsidian strands before wandering over to the second braid. "I didn't know it was possible to feel like this."

Albert paused. Gisela observed his throat tightening as he swallowed. Then he met her gaze. She watched his tongue flicking over his lips, preparing the way for the words that came tumbling out. "From that moment, you showed such kindness and sympathy," his finger traced the hollow at the base of her neck, "something changed within me." He hesitated, gathering his thoughts. "You unlocked something in me, something I believed I would never experience. I don't have words to express this overwhelming..." he trailed off. He looked past her, deep in thought before his attention returned to her. "Of course, there are words for this." Albert smiled, a laugh bubbling at the back of his throat. "I love you, Gisela."

She lay there, his words washing over her. She drifted far away. Present, and yet not. Her mind floated, bringing distance to the sensation of his touch. She felt his finger tracing the hollow in her throat, meandering over her bosom, and somehow the sensation was not touch. Gisela struggled to fathom the incongruity. He was touching her, and yet she floated far distant, unable to actually feel his caress. Then, four words plunged her back into the immediacy of the moment: "I love you, Gisela."

Her ears rang with the intensity in his voice. She floundered in a whirlwind of confused emotions. Love? She didn't know what love was, not really. There were all the fanciful ideas, but nothing anyone ever told her about love matched what she felt in that moment: the desire to have his naked body pressed against hers, wanting to hear him speak again, if only to sense the depth of his emotion when his voice rasped. She felt calm, peace she never dreamed of, just lying there beside this man, her breasts exposed—and that didn't bother her in the least, which she noted with studious curiosity. There was one emotion she did not pay any heed to. In that moment, while she lay beside a man, a part of Gisela's mind sealed off the helpless butterfly of terror fluttering about, frantic inside the confines of cupped hands. His words, "I love you, Gisela" separated her fear even more from the rest of her, until it was subsumed in absolute stillness.

Her silence brought him discomfort. Albert shifted. He lifted his hand, making to withdraw. "I... I want..." He broke off again. His heavy eyebrows drew together, shaping a deep v above the bridge of his nose. Then he laughed, smoothing his features again. "I have never struggled to articulate like this before..."

As he turned away, Gisela clasped his hand. "Maybe we're not meant to speak of it," she whispered. More than words passed between their locked gazes. She lifted his hand and brushed her lips over his fingertips. The gesture sent sparkles coursing through her and pooling in the base of her spine. "I don't have words either," she conceded, lowering her lids, allowing her long, thick lashes to cut short their non-verbal conversation.

In response, he leaned forward and brushed his

lips against her cheekbone. The contact sent another thrill through her. His motion drifted over to her ear, where he stopped to whisper, "I want you to be happy." He planted his lips firmly onto her cheek, then added, "and I want to be there—present in your life." His mouth trailed down her neck to her shoulder. "I want to hear your voice every day." He shifted his weight, pressing his body against hers, hovering his lips beside her own when he said, "I want you, Gisela."

She responded by pressing her mouth to his. Turning towards him, Gisela ignored the scrape of a pebble under her hip. She leaned into him, heart beginning its fluttering dance once more, while her breasts craved his touch. Albert did not wait long to grant her desire. While their kisses became ever more urgent, their tongues teased and probed, and their hands wandered and explored. Heat blazed through her, demanding more. Beyond all capacity for thought, her leg twined between his. She lost herself in the pleasure of his embrace. His hand roved over her thigh and onto her buttock, pulling her closer to him. The rough motion further fanned the flames of her desire.

Then Gisela felt him give way to his own longing. His controlled motions became haphazard and desperate. His mouth was on hers, hot breath brushing against her skin, contrasting the coolness of the air around them. She drifted in a sea of pleasure. His hand between her legs. His fingers drew out her sacred waters, calling forth shivering, tingling ecstasy.

Gisela responded from a place well beyond the reach of reason. His throbbing member crushed into her thigh, bringing awareness of his needs. She moved her hands towards him, pressing against the straining part. The coarseness of his breeches abraded the soft palm of her hand. His moan made her redouble her efforts. Her fingers fumbled on the buttons, and he pushed her hands aside, taking over with deft motions.

Albert strained against her again. She felt silk over iron pressing into her hand. A light touch became more vigorous, and he responded in kind, his fingers working dazzling miracles within her. She arched her back. Her body demanded more. Albert's reply was decisive. He shifted into position between her welcoming, opened legs. He strained against the gates to her paradise, and she moaned his name as she shifted. Albert dove in again, parting the curtain, tantalizing her innermost need. She gasped, knowing that one more thrust would bring the burst of first release, the moment, so long awaited, and which promised even greater, heart-stirring sensations.

Gisela heard a gasp, followed by a cracking twig. The instant her brain came through with both sounds, followed by the clear thought that someone else was privy to her transgression, a bucket of snowmelt poured through her veins. In one fluid reaction, she drew away from Albert, pulling her skirts down over her legs and clutching her blouse over her exposed chest. A heartbeat later, Gisela was popping buttons into place with practised efficiency.

Over the rushing of her blood, she heard the sounds of receding footsteps. She pushed the last button through a hole, pulled herself up and charged out of the concealed hollow without a backward glance. Back on the path, she straightened her skirt, brushing her hands in swift, defined motions to sweep away dead leaves and other debris from the fabric. Her legs moved in long, deliberate strides while she shook twigs and dust out of her hair. Her fingers working dexterously as they wove new braids.

What was I doing? she chided. She swallowed, as thoughts crashed through the veil of her raging hormones. *I just put everything at risk. And for what? What is wrong with me?* She came out into the low-cut wheat stubble remaining after the harvest. Her home loomed into the darkening sky. She glanced at herself once more and knew she could never keep this secret.

Doom settled into her. She dragged herself forward. *What was I thinking? I wasn't thinking at all. That's the problem.* Reaching the fenced-off area, she launched herself over the wooden poles as she did every day, but this time the motion felt uneven. She was disoriented by the overwhelming cocktail of biochemistry coursing through her; however, one thing remained crystal clear. *It is the end of me if anyone finds out.* But how could she keep this secret?

The image of her father's fury, eyes popping out of

his skull, her brothers grunting with exertion to hold him down, hurled icicles through her. Terror held her palpitating heart between its claws and smirked. She stumbled at the corner of the house. Catching herself, she heard a soft, repetitive squeak coming from the porch. Glacial rock replaced her intestines, and she glanced about, hesitant. Should she approach the door and face what was coming? *I have nowhere to run*, she thought. *Better face the consequences and have done with it.* She stood straight, pushed her shoulders back and strode forward, her brow determined and desperation glinting in her cocoa eyes.

She rounded the side of the house and stopped. Her mother sat, head nodding against the backrest of her rocking chair, with a crochet hook hanging limply from her fingers. A ball of yarn lay on the ground a short distance away. The chair swayed and emitted a creak. Gisela stifled a laugh as relief gushed through her. Dizziness tingled behind her eyes, and she reached out to touch the coarse wall of the house, steadying herself.

Father is still busy with the barrels. She smiled. *Of course, he is. It isn't dark yet. They're never done before it's too dark to see in there.*

Her mind illuminated a solution as bright as early morning rays bouncing off the mountain peaks. She stepped lightly up to her mother, placing a hand on her shoulder. "Ma," she whispered. A grunt and a jerk of limbs were followed by fluttering eyelashes. "Ma,"

Gisela soothed. "I'm back, but I'm knackered. Everything's ready for dinner. I'm not hungry. I just want to lie down."

Another grunt. Gisela turned away, so her mother wouldn't see the state of her clothes and hair. "I'll see you in the morning. We can make a nice post-harvest breakfast." Pausing in the doorway, she added, "You know, I think I'll give you a treat. Let me make it."

"Gise," her mother called, but Gisela ignored it, using ponderous steps to signal her passage up the stairs.

23

Hilarion charged ahead, oblivious to trees and shrubs on either side of the gravelly path. The sun hung low in the sky, it's long fingers streaming their gentle caresses through leaves and tree trunks. In the cool of the late afternoon, the forest filled with chatter as its inhabitants went about their business before dark.

He was oblivious to it all. A dense white fog consumed his mind, muffling his senses. It subsumed everything. His strides were uneven. On occasion his disorientation had him knocking his shoulders against branches or tree trunks, or brushing his head too close to a solid object. He even stumbled a few times, catching his balance in the last moment. One hand tugged incessantly at the leather strap slung over his shoulder. Carrying his rifle was once a comfort to him, but now he gripped it with the nervous force of a drowning man. His hand slipped on the smooth leather because it was slick from the sweat pouring off him.

Time ceased. Hilarion was trapped in the void of eternity—the insect trapped in amber to observe the world through a haze of yellow-tinted glasses. The deviation of his perspective, mixed with the haziness brought on by a foggy mind caused dizziness. Everything swirled about him most unnaturally. He threw out a hand to steady himself, only to teeter sideways when he missed the tree he had been aiming for.

His disorientation, did not, however, reach as far as his feet, which found their way home without the help of the conscious mind. He stumbled inside. The four enclosed walls offered a semblance of shelter from the desolation his soul experienced in the forest. He sank to his knees beside his bed, combing his fingers through his hair. Dampness plastered the strands against his skull.

An image of Gisela's enraptured face, her hair forming an ebony nimbus around her features, flashed into his mind. A moment later, his chest constricted. Iron claws squeezed at his ribcage. They were relentless, crushing all life from him. The image of the stranger, the arrogant lord, straining into her accompanied by her gasping moans brought Hilarion's hands onto his ears. He rocked onto his feet, crouching and swaying, his hands clasped to the side of his head.

"No, no, no..." he croaked as he rocked backwards and forwards.

Then, bile surged in green and yellow glory, sweeping away the murkiness clouding his thoughts. Jealousy, combined with the red-hot poker of rage, concocted a bitter brew to scorch his innards as it gushed through him. It was all-consuming. The memory of her rejection. The harshness in her voice. The way she turned her back on him and raced out of sight after his proposal. All of it clubbed him in the stomach. Gisela's rebuffal of his offer had been hard enough to bear, but now she added the indignity of giving herself to another. *Unmarried. Unheeding. Uncaring. She spread her legs without a second thought.*

Agony seared through his chest once more. Black spots flickered across his vision. When it subsided, he noticed his shirt was clammy. It stuck to him, bringing with it the overwhelming sense of defilement. His ardent desire for Gisela now turned into sludge to drag him down. He was contaminated by his enduring wish to be by her side. The leaves of his soul curled with blackened blight. He felt befouled by association. What did his devotion make of him? She gave herself so easily to another. *They barely even met.*

His nails dug into the skin of his head. The twinge bringing respite from the flagellation of his innermost self, the disintegration of everything he held sacred. Hilarion focused on the half-moons pricking around his temples and into his cheeks. Then a thought stabbed through, blinding and coherent. It illuminated the seed of a plan. *She will pay. She MUST pay for this.*

Throughout the night, Hilarion nurtured his strategy to cause as much harm as possible to Gisela. He would ruin any dream she'd ever uttered. Crumbling it all to dust under his righteous fist. By the end of the night, that egg had hatched, but it did not reveal a fledgeling of avian form. The thing Hilarion created in his heart was reptilian, and fire burned at its core.

24

Vincent sat in the hollow, his mind spinning to the music of rustling leaves and chirping birds. His head rested in his hands, elbows propped on his knees. His thoughts swirled through a maze of endless crevasses. The twists and turns took him ever deeper into darker territory where passage was constricted. What should he do?

He wanted Gisela. He wanted to be with her, to share his life with her. Self-doubt raised its monstrous head, bombarding him with scepticism. *How can I possibly be certain? I only met the girl a few times. Is this not more likely a passing craze of the flesh?*

Then the soft voice responded calmly, *she is the one. I don't know how I know, but I know she is everything I have ever wanted.* From there, duty took over. *I cannot do this. My father has already decided. My engagement should have been announced months ago. I promised I would make the commitment to Catherine public upon my return.* His father's stern insistence repeated itself in his own internal voice. *It is my duty.*

Vincent's conscience stood firm, despite the vexing remonstrations he threw at himself. *There is no one else for me. Gisela is the one, and I can be my best with her.*

Best? Disbelief guffawed. *I lie to her. I've kept my true identity from her. And now I claim she brings the best out in me?* It was a ridiculous thought, but still, he persevered. The overwhelming urge to tell her the truth tugged at him, but another urgency was even more prominent. In his mind, he replayed her look of shocked horror. *She left in such a state. She probably won't want to speak to me, or ever wish to see me again, for that matter.* He knew the entire situation had messed up. Everything was turning to ashes and being swept away by the wind.

What should I do?

Oskar, he knew, would be little help on this matter. His best friend's obsession with the fairer sex and playing everyone for all he was worth, was indication enough. Oskar would encourage detachment in line with his "have fun now, don't tie yourself down" policy. *I could never do that,* Vincent acknowledged with a vehement nod. *That would be going against everything I stand for.*

But what was I doing with Gisela anyway? the soft voice asked. There was a hint of reproach in it. Vincent squirmed. He tried to shift his thoughts elsewhere, but he knew he needed to be honest with himself on this.

What had his intentions been? For he could never claim they were pure. His mind revisited the moment he stared down Oskar over Gisela. The altercation came from some unknown depth within him, and the strength of the feeling was unmistakable. *There is more than lust. I feel something for Gisela that cannot be described, and I told her that at least. She will understand the reasons for keeping my identity hidden, but I must come clean. I must tell her.*

Once more he remembered the state in which she left. Her eyes wide, horror etched in her features. Would she even let him approach? Should he go to her father, and put things right by asking for her hand? That would correct their transgression of meeting alone. A sigh expanded from the pit of his stomach rising until it pushed its way past his lips, heavy with the weight of his concerns. He knew nothing could put right what had almost happened.

But she said I should go for it, that she didn't want me to hold back. His own retort was sharp and dripped with disdain. *I should have known better! I should never have allowed it to go that far.* Although his heart ached, he feared he could not right this.

Vincent rose to his feet. The branch swung closed with a crackling swish, hiding the hollow from view, and he turned his back on the place. His hands clenched into fists and unclenched in time to his strides. *What am I going to do?* Oskar was no help, so perhaps Madeleine? What would Madeleine counsel?

With unwavering certainty, Vincent's mind called up Madeleine's face showing disapproval. He flinched inwardly at the flash of her eyes and little lines materialising above the bridge of her nose. Madeleine would be mad at him for leading Gisela on, for keeping secrets from her and for almost ruining her. Rash and indecent, Madeleine would call him. Vincent trembled at the thought of her anger. He knew it would only be worse if she found out someone had witnessed their tryst in the forest.

The observer was the worst part of the whole situation. Who saw them? And what did that person actually see? What would they do?

Knowing he could not find the answers to those questions in the moment, Vincent returned his wayward thoughts to Gisela and whether he should seek her out immediately. He needed to talk to her—that, at least, was clear. How to do it? She would be surrounded by her family. Could he march up and insist on speaking with her? *No, that will draw even more attention to her. Getting her into trouble won't help me. She won't want to listen to me then. I must think this through.*

Vincent changed route and headed towards the village. He was oblivious to his guard five paces behind who looked up several times, opening his mouth, but then shutting it again. Vincent was occupied by his own thoughts and heeded nothing else.

Better to speak with her in the morning, Vincent

thought. He knew he could find a way. He had to find a way. Things came so easily to him when he was in her presence. It would flow, once he saw her. How to do it though? That was the difficulty he could not resolve. Each thought took him deeper and deeper into a pit of his own making, and there appeared to be no way out of it. Vincent headed straight to his screened-off quarters. He refused to see or speak to anyone. Instead, he nursed his apprehensions through a fitful night's sleep where nothing formulated itself. No seed. No egg. Nothing.

25

Gisela roused herself when sounds filtered up from below. She sat with her back leaning against the closed door to her room, her legs pulled up against her chest. She lifted her face from her hands. *I cannot change what is done*, she thought. She listened to the voices rumbling in conversation. One of her brothers laughed, and she stood, heading to the dresser. While loneliness washed over her, she brushed her hair with vigorous strokes. The walls around her grew thicker. The air in the room was heavy—oppressive.

What am I going to do? What can I do? There was nothing. She had no power. She was stuck, as always, waiting for others to decide for her. *What will Hilarion do?* she wondered. There was no doubt in her mind that the gasp and hurriedly retreating steps were Hilarion's. *How can I be so certain? It could have been anyone.* She shook her head, swiping away the rejoinder with a furious brushstroke against her shimmering locks. The tangles in her hair came away, but her scalp stung from the tugging motion. *I know it was Hilarion.* In darkened silence, she mulled over Hilarion and what he'd seen —what he must think. Her face burned at the thought. *Shame, shame, shame!* her thoughts chided.

Should I really feel shame? Albert feels so right. He makes me feel whole. Now he wasn't near, the loneliness crashed over her, a suffocating wave that pushed her to the edge of reason. *Albert is my reason,* she thought. *The up to my down, right to my wrong. He is everything. Surely the dragon gods would not wish me to feel shame for something so right. They must understand and forgive, even if humans can't. Albert is my reason,* she reiterated.

Another thought sparked into existence. *Dragons. Hilarion. Did they send him to stop me? If Albert and I continued, I would have lost my status as their representative in the festival. I could not, with dignity, continue as Harvest Queen.* From there, her thoughts tumbled over each other. Relief mixed with gratitude. *It is the will of the gods that I dance, and they saved me from my trespass with Albert, but they do not disapprove, for they sent their message through Hilarion, my protector and friend. He will keep the secret. And I can speak with Albert tomorrow or the day after.*

Her mind turned to the man who flipped her world

upside down. She thought on her decision to take him to the forest hollow. *It is strange how overwhelming the desire to take him there was. What was that all about?* She thought for a moment. *It is as though I wished to experience love, just once. To give myself over to him precisely because I love him, but I know Father is choosing someone else for me. Albert said he loves me, that he wants to be with me.* Her thoughts flitted to her father's delight at several marriage proposals. *Would he contemplate Albert? That's just wishful thinking. Oh Albert,* she mused. *We could make each other happy, couldn't we?*

She was transported back to that moment in the stillness of the living forest, a breeze stirring in the leaves, birds chirping and hopping among the branches. Two hearts beating in a harmonious rhythm, blending into a song of love. She heard his whispered words again, *I never felt this way before.... I love you.* Gisela trailed her finger down her neck and over her throat, downward until it hit the resistance of her bodice. There, her inner realist interrupted with its own sentiment. *He could have been lying. Perhaps Albert only said those things to make me more pliable.*

She sent the hairbrush flying across the room where it thudded against the wooden wall. Every fibre in her body rejected the thought. *No, no, no! It is the truth. Albert loves me. I know it, just like I know it was Hilarion who saw us.*

A knock came at her door. Gisela spun around at

the sound. "Gise, dear, are you sure you don't want any dinner?" her mother's voice drifted through to her.

Gisela took in her appearance in a quick appraisal. The leaves and twigs were removed from her hair, but her bodice was still buttoned haphazardly. There were stains on her skirts and dirt on her arms. "I'm going to bed," she said with firm resolve. "I'll see you in the morning, Ma."

"What's going on, Gise? You've been so different lately."

Her stomach clenched, but she brushed over the sense of guilt with a light tone. "It's nothing, Ma."

There was a long pause. Then her mother said, "When you're ready to talk, I'm here. I'll be waiting."

Gisela bit her lip. "It's really nothing. Good night, Ma."

"Sleep well then, love."

Gisela listened to the footsteps receding. She waited until she heard the creak of the last step. The conversation below her shifted, and with it she turned her awareness inward once more. *Albert loves me*, she reiterated as the unbuttoned dress crumpled to the floor. She stepped over to the wash stand and the airy sensation of her shift intensified her focus on her own body. The way her breasts felt, freed from the confines of the bodice. They hung in perfect balance and swung lightly in tune with her motions. The cold water tingled against the skin of her arms and legs, heightening the contrast with heat searing in other places. Pulling the shift up to her stomach, Gisela gasped when the cool cloth came into contact with her lady parts. Any remnant of restraint disintegrated before the onslaught of her unsatiated desire.

The rush of memories was swift and decisive. She relived his kisses, the caresses that brought her all-consuming flame to life. Her shift tumbled to the floor next, atop the discarded, damp cloth. While Gisela's hands explored the softer and harder parts of her figure, she reclined on her bed. She lost herself in the memories of Albert's lips and the sensations he called forth with ease. Her fingers followed the trail he had left in her mind, plunging into the darkened depths she'd only vaguely been aware of hitherto. She trailed up through the curtain and found the hardened peak above.

Past and present aligned. Gisela fell out of time while she responded to the deep need of her body, a need which had been left wanting. Her whole being strained for the release Albert had promised her, but circumstances had stolen away in a cruel jest. Her fingers called forth the sweet nectar which had lain dormant her whole life, awaiting a moment such as this. Tingles followed on sparkles and radiant flashes of electrifying thrills. With one final thrust, Gisela shuddered in ecstasy.

Her senses returned as though an oil lamp had

been lit in a dark room. She heard her family talking over dinner. She saw the shadowy contours of her room. She felt dampness on the quilt beneath her and she tasted the dryness of her mouth. Gisela fumbled in the dark to extricate the damp cloth she had used earlier from below her discarded shift. She felt the cool, wet patch on the shift and sighed. After completing her ablutions, she rummaged in the cupboard, in the dark. Awareness of her nakedness intensified, and she hurried to pull a clean shift into place.

For once, her thoughts were still. Gisela slipped into a deep and restful sleep, abandoning her worries. That clamouring babble could wait until the morrow.

During the night, the wind picked up. It tugged and played with a square of light wool. In the moonlight, the wind pulled its dance-partner among the leaves, where the green shawl cavorted with the branches, changing hands every so often until the first partner reclaimed it. Together, the wind and the shawl whirled higher and higher, admiring the brilliant stars that illuminated their path. At long last, just before dawn, the wind subsided, abandoning its plaything in a highland pasture. The discarded trifle quivered feebly, its silent protests unheeded. Within hours, it would be trampled beyond recognition by the passage of several hundred cows and sheep who were herded down the mountain for their autumn and winter stabling in the valley. No one ever noticed the missing green shawl, nor did anyone see the mud-encrusted strip of fabric in the mountains as anything worthy of attention. Forgotten, abandoned, the shawl would never tell its tale.

26

Hilarion woke calmer but no less determined. The wyvern which had hatched in his heart the previous evening, flexed in anticipation. Its steely eyes were trained on the task at hand and Hilarion almost skipped with fiendish glee for the moment when he unmasked the lord and his dealings with Gisela.

The surge of energy he'd experienced at the thought of accompanying his first hunt since becoming gamekeeper was nothing in comparison to the hell-fire intensity he now felt. Hilarion bounded out the impoverished hovel without a thought for breakfast. Revenge was his sustenance now and he savoured this flavourful ale. Darkness in his heart, tinted his sight and turned the tree-covered landscape monochrome. He had no thoughts for the day or signs of life within it. Hilarion was a bloodhound on a trail and he spared his regard for nothing else.

On the outskirts of the village, in a huge field (bordered, as was customary, by a row of trees), men and women congregated in small groups. Tents were being hoisted. The heavy thudding of a mallet against a stake reverberated. Laughter bubbled in the air which tingled with mounting excitement. Hilarion was oblivious to it all. He strode past without a care for the acquaintances who called to him. He was so absorbed in his task, no distraction could penetrate deep enough to catch his attention. *Find the lord. Follow him discreetly. Observe and identify a way to unmask him.*

He reached the inn without interference. Some of the lord's men were milling outside, but there were too few and their voices ricocheted over to where he stood, grating and discordant. The time he spent in their company the day before, served him well now. He knew they did not speak like that when their lord was near.

Hilarion sauntered over to the group of people closest to the door. His nonchalant air belied the taut bowstring tensing his muscles. He listened in on the conversation, but his sniffer-dog-brain passed over it in a breath. Gossip about the stable-hand and his tryst with the barmaid did not interest Hilarion in the slightest. He joined the outskirts of the group, feigning interest while casting a glance towards the inn. There wasn't much going on inside either.

One of the lower servants in the lord's entourage recognised Hilarion who acknowledged the man's greeting with a nod and a grunt. Hilarion went further. With a grimace, he asked, "Looking forward to the festival?"

The gruff utterance startled the others, but then they shifted their topic of conversation and clamoured over each other about the food and the women and the dancing. Several referred to an angel in ruby skirts. Hilarion assumed they meant Gisela and added, "She'll only be dancing tomorrow. It is custom for the Harvest Queen to only perform after her investiture."

There was more grumbling, and then Hilarion's attention was grabbed by a movement at the doorway. He observed two figures slip out of the inn. The first was dressed in drab brown clothes, the second in grey with a bright red neckerchief. The sight of them brought his eyes close together. There was something off about those two. Something didn't quite fit. He began to move away from the group he was in and noticed a third man leaving the inn. This one was burly and moved with poise. The fluidity of his movements set another bell ringing in Hilarion's mind. *This definitely stinks. They look like they're up to something fishy,* he thought.

When the third man tailed the other two, Hilarion started to put things together. He noted the last man's clothes were worn and patched in places. It brought into sharp contrast how new the other men's clothes were. They didn't even have stains on them. Hilarion followed as his mind sparked onto the answer. The relatively tall man in brown, who was quiet, had to be the lord in his disguise. Hilarion even recognised the man's back, which bubbled a flood of pitch through his veins at the memory from his last encounter with that posterior. His memory flickered back to Gisela's face and how she surrendered herself to the man Hilarion now followed. Raven-winged murder glanced his mind with rustling feathers, but the wyvern burned the thought to a crisp, drawing Hilarion back to the bodyguard who strode behind the other two men. He realised he was too close and dropped back, feigning interest in the potter's shop window. In the interim, he tried to still the seething mass of his blood.

Following the three men all day, Hilarion understood he would be hard-pressed to come close to the lord. Unless the lord slipped away from his bodyguard, Hilarion knew he could not get close to the man. His patience stretching to breaking point, Hilarion continued the task he set himself, roaming through the festival ground, watching the disguised lord lending a hand here or there to set up. His pretence made Hilarion bristle. How dare this fop with his butter-soft hands and pampered childhood pretend to be a labourer, a man of honour and hard work? Hilarion scoffed at the affront. How could this lordling who never did an honest day's work be allowed to slum it with the commoners, just for his entertainment? The realisation egged Hilarion's determination further. He would bring this arrogant man down and repay every insult he'd dared to dole out. Hilarion grimaced at a bitter taste of chicory, which accompanied the memory of the lord's cold dismissal a few weeks before.

Evening fell, and the disguised men slipped away from the frantic crowd. Fires sent sparks into the darkening sky and a group of musicians played a merry tune, which was drowned out by the hubbub of laughter and raucous voices. Hilarion, never once allowing himself rest, saw the three figures making their unhurried way in the direction of the town. He trailed behind them and observed the lord and his companion disappearing into the inn while the third man leaned against the outer wall as he cleaned his fingernails with the tip of a sharp knife. It gleamed dully in the light of the moon. Hilarion hung back. The shadows served him well, as did the distraction of music and voices drifting from the field behind him.

A short while later, a throng of attendants pushed out into the night. A moment passed, and then the lord and his companion stepped into the bright light spilling from the doorway. Hilarion squinted at the changed men. Both now shone in finery, and Hilarion was taken aback by the difference, even though he'd been expecting it. Caught off-guard, he pressed himself into a shadowy doorway as the company passed by him. He glimpsed the lord, his short sword swinging from his hip. The sight of the aristocrat among his people made Hilarion almost reject his own knowledge. This man was so different from the friendly, laughing worker Hilarion had trailed all day. However, the reptilian transformation his heart had undergone the evening before did not grant him the opportunity to deliberate on that observation further. Instead, he turned and followed the group to continue his observations.

It was late when Hilarion slipped into the forest. While he journeyed to his home, he worked out the final details of the plot he had spun over the course of the evening. He was certain he could achieve his ultimate purpose on the next day.

27

Vincent woke uncertain and with trepidation. Any resolve he felt to speak with Gisela and clear the air between them evaporated in his fruitless night. His uncertainties redoubled, and having no one to confide in made his reluctance to find Gisela even more pronounced. In the end, he pushed the fussy voice of his conscience back into the walled confines of his subconscious mind and set off with Oskar to enjoy a day filled with fun and laughter. The physical exertions he participated in helped lift his spirits, and soon Vincent felt reinvigorated.

In the evening, they returned to the inn for Vincent to change. He knew it would be important to attend the opening night of the festival in all the finery of his aristocratic bearing. On his way through the darkened streets, accompanied by his retinue, Vincent sensed a shadowy figure in an alley. His first instinct was to have the scoundrel rounded up and disposed of, but then he thought making a fuss would draw too much attention, and he wanted to keep as low a profile as possible under the circumstances. Vincent promptly forgot about the man in the shadows and turned his attention to the entertainment of the evening.

A large field on the outskirts of the village was the customary grounds for Ylvaton's harvest festival. Tents mushroomed throughout the space, filling the air with scents and sounds. People shouted their bawdy comments above the hubbub of conversation at tables where ale flowed freely. A ball hit a tower of hollowed, wooden cylinders, collapsing the pyramidal construction with a resounding crash. Lanterns flickered, pronouncing the shadows beyond their illuminated haloes. An accordion stretched and contracted as it engendered the bright strains of a dance tune in a distant area of the field. From between two tents, Vincent caught sight of whirling skirts and flailing limbs close to where the music emanated.

He became acutely aware of his status as a lord. Now, when he passed, people stopped talking and some even bowed. He missed the camaraderie from earlier in the afternoon where he was a part of the crowd. As a lord, he stood out, and that deepened his solitude in a throng of people. For all the times he had felt isolated from the world around him, he had never experienced it quite as cutting as in that moment. The mayor tottered up to share some pleasantries with

Vincent and Oskar, but soon he was called off to attend to another group of new arrivals.

Finding a good vantage point to observe the goings on, Vincent seated himself, resting his hand on the hilt of his sword. He proceeded to scan the area. Although he knew very well that Gisela had no intention of coming to the festival on that evening, her absence annoyed him. The thoughts he had dismissed earlier in the day resurged with greater force while he sat in detached silence—nobleman among the commoners. Vincent fidgeted with the end of a tablecloth while he pondered once more his dilemma with Gisela.

Oskar roused him from his reverie with a forceful slap on the shoulder. "No time for brooding, Vince, my friend. Come, you only live once, and I can see several fine sets of hips swaying to the music."

Vincent stood, but shook his head in answer to Oskar. Then he turned and strode away in the direction of the village.

"You're no fun!" Oskar shouted after him, and added for good measure, "I'll have a romp for both of us then."

Vincent swatted his hand in Oskar's general direction and kept walking. He sensed his bodyguard a few paces behind him. In the comfortable silence and darkness beyond the fairground, Vincent glanced up at the cloudless canopy. *Diamonds*, he thought at the sight of the myriad twinkling stars. *Gisela deserves to be like the night sky, bejewelled with diamonds.*

28

Gisela spent her day immersed in a fuzzy cloud. There was something surreal about performing her mundane tasks. She was changed and it felt strange to her that no one noticed. Everything continued as though nothing were different, and yet, she felt transformed. She almost giggled at the thought of her parents, oblivious to the initiation she underwent on the evening before.

Her amusement was short-lived, though. She soon returned to her standard activity of pondering what she should do. She longed to escape her chores and run into the village to see the preparations for the festival, but Gisela knew that was just a pretence. What she really wanted, more than anything, was to speak with Albert. She knew she had to. Something told her it was imperative she did so, and still, she put off doing it. She avoided it because everything felt awkward. The transgression from the afternoon before weighed even more heavily on her in the blinding light of day. She felt with mounting certainty that the circumstances changed the delicate balancing act of their relationship.

There was also Hilarion to contemplate. What would he do? Would he act on what he saw? Should she go and speak with him? Would that alert her parents? Or would he do what she believed was the gods bidding and forgive her transgression? She knew she had to be careful so her father would remain oblivious to her escapade on the previous day. What should she do? Was there anything she could do?

Gisela continued over-thinking her dilemma until the sun set. Uncomfortable in the presence of her family, terrified someone would notice something different about her, Gisela wolfed down her food and excused herself. "Mrs Smith said I should rest well for tomorrow. I'll go and lie down now."

Seeing her mother purse her lips, Gisela recognised the motion and knew an objection was forthcoming. "I'm feeling quite tired, and I really want to be at my best for tomorrow's performance. I wouldn't want to let everyone down."

Before her mother could formulate a counterargument, Gisela hastened to clear her plate and hurried upstairs. She breathed a sigh of relief when she reached her room without either of her parents commenting.

The agitated chirping of birds woke Gisela. Light filtered through small cracks in the outer wall and when she sat up, she shivered from the chill early-morning air. She sat still for a moment, bracing herself before swinging her legs over the side. The cool floor-boards tingled against her bare feet. A thought struck her as she straightened, and she sat back down again with a solid rock-like lump replacing her stomach.

It is festival day. Letting out a breath in a slow, steady stream, Gisela stood again. "Oh my," she murmured. "This is it!" Then she allowed an excited shriek to burst forth, accompanied by a swarm of butterflies bursting from the unwinding core at the pit of her stomach. She jetéd across the room, flung open the door of her cupboard and pulled out a clean shift and dress.

In no time she was ready, her hair brushed to gleaming obsidian and her shoes polished until they reflected her face back at her. Gisela pranced down the stairs, the kaleidoscope of butterflies still causing turmoil in her innards. As always, her mother stood in the kitchen producing a cloud of hunger-eliciting fragrances. Gisela's father sat by the table, a thick ledger spread out before him where he noted down details of the collected harvest.

Gisela chirped her good mornings. Both stopped their tasks. Her father rose and pulled her into a tight hug. She nestled into his embrace, squeezing back with her arms.

"Did you sleep well?" her mother asked, also slipping her arms around Gisela.

She nodded. "Yes, and I'm ready for today—as ready as I'll ever be." She laughed a peal of crystal bells. Then, she stepped back, took her mother's hand and asked, "Is there anything I can do this morning, Ma?"

Her father's approving glance caught her gaze before he settled back into his chair and continued scratching at the parchment with his ink and quill. Gisela chatted with her mother. Her voice bubbled with exuberance as it hadn't done in many months. Everything seemed so much brighter on this morning. The whole world held its breath, awaiting her big moment later that afternoon. Meanwhile, she breathed in the scent of eggs and roasting bread.

The bottom stair creaked and Gisela beamed up at her brother, Robert. "What is all this commotion about?" he grumbled.

"I'm going to dance today," Gisela said, flouncing over to where he now sat by the table. She leaned over it, giving him a meaningful look.

"What's for breakfast?"

Unable to bite back a sigh, Gisela's eyes rolled heavenward.

"Scrambled eggs and toast," her mother cut in, checking the bickering before it started. "And you could give her some words of encouragement. Gise has worked hard for this. The least you can do is show some interest."

"She gets more than enough attention without me. The whole town is interested in Gisela these days. Can I have my breakfast now?"

Gisela dropped a plate in front of Robert with a loud clatter, spilling dribbles of egg onto the table.

"Robert... Gisela," their father reprimanded. He did not lift his head. His quill kept scratching against the parchment for a while longer as she and her brother exchanged a sizzling glare. Then, accompanied by the rustling sound of parchment, Mr Winry gathered up his ledger and writing utensils. "Where is Sven?" he asked as he stowed the items in a chest near the fireplace in the adjoining living space.

"Still sleeping," Robert mumbled past a mouthful of egg.

"You stayed out late last night," his mother reproached.

"But Ma, it's the festival! Of course we stayed out late."

Gisela huffed, and stormed towards the front door. "I'll see to the sheep," she said in annoyance.

She strode to the barn, seething. *Stupid Robert. He always has to go and ruin my good mood. Why did he and Sven have permission to go to the festival yesterday?* "So unfair!" she exclaimed.

Once she had tended the sheep and led the draft

horse to pasture, Gisela felt better. She was never able to stay angry with Robert for long, and it was the day of her debut. She would dance like never before, and she tingled with anticipation.

A few hours later, she walked down the lane towards the village, but for a change, she was accompanied by her whole family. They were all dressed in their finest clothes. It took all of Gisela's self-control to remain composed and walk with poise. All she wanted was to run ahead, laughing and calling out to anyone she met that she'd be performing as Harvest Queen later. While she walked, the butterflies in her stomach contorted into a solid mass once more. Trepidation and excitement concocted an unusual blend within her. *Can I really do this? Am I ready for this privilege? Am I going to bumble it all up and ruin the festival?*

Her mother's gentle hand on her shoulder drew her awareness back to the outside world. With a soft smile, her mother eased her fears. She gently patted Gisela's arm and whispered, "It will be all right, little sprite. You will be spectacular."

Sounds drifted to them on the air. It was a level of noise Gisela had come to associate with the harvest festival. Strains of folk music were overpowered by raucous laughter and people shouting above the hubbub of many smaller conversations. Banners fluttered in the wind and on occasion an unfastened tent flap slapped a repetitive beat. The air hummed with hard-working people relaxing and having fun in the wake of summer toils.

Gisela strolled arm in arm with her mother. They passed some booths and then Mrs Winry stopped to chat with a neighbour who was selling baked goods. Gisela glanced about, but they had already lost track of her father and brothers. As she craned her neck in search of her family, she saw Albert. He was walking towards her with great strides, his jaw set and a determined gleam in his eyes. She stepped closer to him, closing the distance between them. His presence washed over her and she paid no heed to the other people around them.

The intensity of Albert's gaze burned, and before he reached her, he said fervently, "Gisela, I must speak with you... away from all these people." She hesitated. A part of her brain questioned whether that was wise. "There is something I must tell you," he urged. "It is very important."

Gisela felt the earnestness in his voice calling to her core. He was agitated and her whole being wanted to assuage the upheaval he experienced. She took his hand, ready to slip between the tents, when a sharp voice cut through the milling throng with a single word, suspending her in the terror of discovery.

"Gisela!" her father called.

She looked at Albert, her eyes wide. She dropped his hand as though it burned her. "I'll find you—after the dancing. Just go." Then she turned and strode to where she'd heard her father's voice. "Yes, Father?"

His hand fell onto her shoulder, claws gripping into her. "Who was that man?"

"What man, father?" she winced at how her voice trembled.

"The one you were talking to. Who is he?"

Gisela blinked, willing herself to remain calm. "He just wanted to know when the dance performance starts."

Dark eyes bored into her and she felt heat rising up her neck and to her cheeks. She hoped beyond hope her father would not notice how her hand quivered.

"Ah! There you are!" Mrs Winry exclaimed. "You won't believe what happened to Mrs Fenworth..."

Mr Winry turned his attention away from Gisela, who took the opportunity to link arms with her mother again and allow Mrs Winry's words to wash over her while she thought on her situation. Before long, Gisela noted the sun glowing orange on its descent beyond the mountains. She turned to her parents and smiled. "It is time. I'll go and join Mrs Smith and the other dancers in preparation for the procession."

"You go ahead, dear," her mother said as she hugged her.

Mr Winry nodded but said nothing.

While she picked her way to the group of dancers assembling around Mrs Smith near the raised, wooden stage, she wondered how she could get away and speak with Albert. *It seemed quite important,* she thought. *But father doesn't trust me, and he will never allow it. What am I going to do?*

A shadow fell over her. Gisela looked up to find Albert striding beside her. He looked straight ahead, as though it were pure coincidence he was walking beside her. His face was a perfect study of impassivity. She dropped her gaze and pretended he wasn't there.

"Gisela," he said. His voice was low and taut with emotion. "I... I kept something from you, and I must tell you everything. You deserve to know me properly, and I want... I don't want to keep secrets from you." They neared the group of dancers and Gisela slowed down, just enough so he could finish. "I have to go now," he continued. "I will be sure to tell you after your performance ends. Good luck, my love. I know you are going to be amazing."

Before she could think of anything to say to reassure him, he slipped in among the crowd, and she lost sight of him. Moments later, she was swept into a whirl of preparations: where to stand in the procession, what to say, how to address the lord (for surely he would wish to congratulate her once the dance ended). The list of things she needed to remember went on and on until Gisela felt dizzy. Her mind thrummed with all the instructions she'd been given at such short notice. As she spoke, Mrs Smith herded the group of dancers out into the lane.

They stopped, and Mrs Smith called out, "Places!"

The other ten girls, all younger than Gisela by several years, lined up behind her. The harvest sceptre, a heavy wooden rod, curved at the top, carved with leaves and with a cornucopia shaped at the base of the curve was handed to her. The musicians stood in readiness beside them, and they waited. At first, Gisela didn't understand why. Then the reason struck her.

The lord hasn't arrived yet.

The sun almost touched the horizon when the crowd in the festival field quietened. Gisela could make out a procession reaching the stage. A rotund man hopped up onto the platform and from his voice, she knew it was the mayor. *That must mean we are almost ready.* Sure enough, a moment later, the first elongated note emanated from the accordion. It was accompanied by a sweet trill from a fife and soft strains on a fiddle. Gisela's feet moved, but she felt distant, out of control. She led the procession past all the onlookers. Her mind floated in a dim bubble, aware of the people around her and noting, absent-mindedly, that there were around ten times as many as she was used to from rehearsals. She glided onto the stage and turned to face the crowd. She felt the last warming rays of the sun stroking her back before the ruby disk dipped under the horizon, leaving only her with her blazing crimson skirts to brighten the heavens.

Then, the moon rose from the tall peaks on the horizon. It was pale with the pink hue of early autumn.

Harvest moon, she thought as it ascended into view beyond the spectators who stood with their faces upturned—all waiting for her. "Welcome to Ylvaton," Gisela intoned. "The harvest is achieved. May your stores be plentiful and the coming winter, mild. Today we celebrate the culmination of our labours. We hope you may set your hearts at ease and find enjoyment in this entertainment we offer."

Gisela handed the staff down to Mrs Smith, who stood below her. Taking her place in the centre of the group, she felt a numbness spreading through her from her fingertips and toes gathering closer to her heart with every short breath. The sea of upturned faces made the paralysis more pronounced. Her thoughts raced at ten times the speed, making the lethargy in her limbs all the more noticeable.

She shut her eyes. Cutting off the light brought her into the stillness of the dark. *Breathe*, she instructed. *Breathe, Gisela*. The memory of the warm sun prickled against her skin and she felt the radiant glow of the moon illuminating everything she was. The moon smiled down at her, and Gisela felt time converge on that pinprick moment. Everything she was, everything she had ever been and all the possibility of the endless universe gathered into her. *Breathe.*

Focus, she thought as she flexed her hand. One heel rose until she stretched onto the ball of her foot. The motion grounded her. Her back straightened. She felt the beat of her heart. It was fast, but strong and steady. *Focus.*

The musicians changed the tune in a fluid transition. *Listen.* Her whole body strained in the suspension between waiting and starting into motion. The tune filled every fibre of her being. It regulated her heart and, then, subsumed her. The music became the very reason for her existence. There was nothing else. She became the expression of the tune. It was her, she was it and it whirled her through the turmoil of her emotions, those doubts, fears, hopes and wishes—everything fell away. With the energy of the other dancers whirling about her, Gisela rose above it all and became the tip of the arrow. They were the bow, the means for her ascent—and she was grateful. She was not alone. Every dancer who ever existed stood by her now, lifting her and showing her the glory of this calling. Beyond them, twined above her in the gathering darkness of the sky, she made out the silvery shapes of her gods. Liquid bodies shimmered as bright claws gestured towards her and gleaming eyes encouraged her to take her first step.

Muscles shifted. What was still, became motion. Freedom. Gisela trusted her being and surpassed all physical restraints. There was no thought—only action. Where she had tried before, now she did—with superb execution. Everything was fluid. She allowed herself to become one with the flow. For once, she trusted herself explicitly. She let go of doubt. Cast self-criticism to the wind. Left fear behind.

When she leapt, she sensed the myriad connections around her. She felt herself become part of the breath, filling life with meaning and hope. She transcended the petty difficulties of her own existence, her own time. The web of people training their attention on her, the whirl of her companions surrounding her, the air shared on everyone's breath, the music caressing every ear—they were all bound together in this moment. Exquisite and transient.

29

Vincent stood, mouth agape. He needed to reassess his idea of a good dancer. Gisela took everything to a new plane. Her artistry had grown since the last time he watched her dance just a few days before. He could not take his eyes off her. He was oblivious to the other dancers around her, but now a new dimension was added. In the glow of the full moon, she transformed into something otherworldly. Her movements were as precise as always, perfectly executed, but they expanded into something else, something beyond dance.

Gisela became one with the music. She whirled. Her crimson skirts billowed about her like flames. Tension crackled in the air about her, and the scent of magnolias drifted to Vincent on the air. His mind paused at the contradiction of that fragrance with the time of year, but then it opened up to the possibility.

Vincent shrugged, accepting the discrepancy. He watched, eyes opened wide, as Gisela launched herself into the sky once more.

The dark heavens blazed with the fiery garments that formed a tail to match the graceful wings of her arms. For a split second, and in a blaze of glory, the woman he loved transformed into a phoenix. She became the living symbol of life and destruction. Fingers stretching into fanned-out wing-tips blessed the gathering of people in the shadows below. Diamond-glinting stars above converged on her, becoming a glittering crown. She converted to light. She blazed and the spectators were forced to shield their eyes. Still, Vincent could not take his gaze off her. She captured him, captivated all minds, and only she could decide when to set them free. She was golden. Peace radiated from her—a gift from the firebird. Tranquillity settled into almost every soul.

The musicians continued the melody, although they paid no heed to their own playing. They, too, had become a part of the magic of the moment. The tune rang out more powerful than mere instruments could produce and Vincent had the feeling the mountains and the forest were contributing to the song in some deep, meaningful way he could not quite grasp. Her foot alighted on the stage and stillness enveloped her. Gisela became a study in the moment in which the last note rings out and silence follows. No one could move. Every spectator there was bewitched by the magnitude of her performance. Everyone knew what they had seen should have been impossible and, yet, they had witnessed it.

With the spell broken, Vincent strode forward. He wanted to pull her into his arms, confess everything he kept secret from her, and ask her the one thing that had overtaken all others in importance. Then he realised he was dressed in his fine aristocratic apparel. The light silk shirt and the beautiful embroidered cloak weighed on him. He wished to tear them from him and cast them in the dirt, but he refrained. Instead, he slipped into the darkened space between two tents and quickly stripped them off to reveal his peasant garb underneath.

He hoped his possessions were well-enough hidden, for he could not wait. Something drove him forward to confront Gisela and lay his heart bare to her. The cheering crowd became a soft buzz to his dazed ears. He saw the light of his life curtsey as though from a long distance. His mind raced faster than his body ever could. The natural motions of his physical form appeared disembodied and lethargic to him. It was too slow. He needed to be beside her, and there was still a significant distance between them. He was oblivious to her speech. The sound of her voice washed over him, but he couldn't fathom what she said. He hurtled forward and came to an abrupt halt beside the stairs to the stage. In the same instant, Gisela stepped onto the first stair. Her gaze rested on him and she beamed, her smile reaching deep into her eyes, but then her attention flickered as she caught sight of something else behind Vincent. Dread invaded her features and Vincent spun around to see what caused her such terror.

30

As the dancing began, Hilarion moved in the direction of the lord who stood near the stage. Hilarion had no thought for anything except his target. Gisela's magnificent performance ensnared everyone else, but he was oblivious. The hard basalt casing around his heart would have splintered and disintegrated like an exfoliation dome if he had glanced up to receive the blessing of life and love Gisela bestowed on those who watched. Instead, the reptilian fixation consumed all his thoughts, turning him blind and deaf to all else.

When the lord slipped through the crowd unnoticed because all eyes were still captivated by Gisela, Hilarion followed. His teeth showed in a feral smile when he saw the lord slip into the space between two tents. Blood rushed in his ears, blocking out all other sound. He crept forward and waited in the shadows. A triumphant gleam sparked to life in his deep-set eyes when the man, now dressed as a commoner, withdrew from the darkened area beside the tents. The disguised lord strode forward, his attention on the brightly lit stage and not sparing a glance for the shadows near him.

Hilarion darted into the dimness. His eyes took a moment to adjust and then he saw a pile of fabric hastily discarded on the ground. He scooped up the clothes. The soft caress of silk on his hands meant nothing to him beyond the thought, *Now she'll regret everything!* His heart soared on leathery bat-wings, plunging the night into deeper, more sinister darkness. As he turned, his toe brushed against something hard. He stooped again, his free hand investigating in the gloom. There was a clank of metal against metal as his fingers clasped around the cool haft of a sword. It was heavy, but he hefted it without difficulty.

Emerging from the darkened area between the tents, Hilarion fixed his gaze on his next victim. Gisela stood, her hair billowing about her, a gleaming copy of the night sky above. He did not see her beauty. He was blind to the virtuous flame blazing in her eyes, oblivious to the serenity she exuded. Hilarion did notice an essence of flame emanating from her—bright and life-giving. The shade of her skirts, still winging from her vigorous motions, segued into the image of fire in a perfect transition.

His eyes returned his own fire to match hers, but he

thought, *If she is the flame, then I am the smoke.* He envisioned billowing clouds of soot streaming from him, a cloak to envelop and smother the woman on the stage above him. The wind of his thoughts lent him wings and he glided forward through the crowd, oblivious to the tumultuous clapping and cheering. He advanced in a daze of tunnel vision. It could have been a starless night, for all the light his eyes perceived. Darkness consumed him and obscured everything around him into shades of black. The only colour to pierce this self-inflicted twilight was Gisela's flame.

He jostled the lord in commoner's clothing and trod the first step rising towards Gisela's vantage on the stage. Hilarion shouted with a thunderous voice, carrying across the crowd and hushing all instantly, "My, do I have a surprise for you, slut!" He took another step and gestured grandly to the man behind him. The cloak he held draped over his arm billowed out in a rich violet cloud. "May I introduce you to—His Lordship!" Hilarion's lips curled in a smile when he heard the gasp from the gathered crowd, but there was no humour in his eyes. "I just watched this man, whom you were getting so intimately acquainted with day before yesterday, leave these items behind the tent over there." Again the arm waved, drawing attention to the belongings Hilarion held. "And you," he continued, rounding on Gisela once more and taking another menacing step towards her, "you really took the piss with this bloke, you sket. What did his lordship 'ave to offer you, other than his hard cock? I expect he made sweet promises he never expected or cared to keep, but I caught you out, I did. I saw you give yourself to this man. And what has he offered in return? Can he restore your good name? He probably promised you wedding bells, but of course, he has no intention of fulfilling such a promise. He'll leave you in the gutter where you belong. Skank! You are not worthy of the position you've been elevated to. Whore! You are no queen, and you have no right to represent Ylvaton today."

A murmur rippled out behind him, but Hilarion was fixated on Gisela. He saw her eyes glint—dewdrops on hard rock. *Yes,* he thought. *Be angry, but you cannot undo what you've done. Your tears may serve you though. Be contrite and beg for forgiveness, and maybe I'll be indulgent to your plight. Although, you don't deserve my compassion at all.*

31

Gisela's mouth became a desert. Hot, dry air parched her tongue and seared it to the base of her throat. Words caught, shrivelled and died there. Her eyes were locked on Hilarion. His words echoed around her, and she heard the crowd respond, a rustling whisper of leaves through a forest. There was nothing she could do now. The whole valley would know her supposed fall soon enough. Just as the wind blew through the whole forest—caressing tree after tree, leaf after leaf—she knew no one would pass up on the gossip Hilarion had just offered. It was irrelevant that he was basing his accusation on a misunderstanding. *Or was it?*

Her gaze flicked to the man she knew as Albert. His eyes were fixed on her, pleading. Guilt racked his features. She saw him try to speak, but he seemed as paralysed as she felt. Although, she detected a light within him. *It isn't true! None of it is true! Or most of Hilarion's take, at least.* Gisela felt certainty warm deep within her belly. *Albert had no intention of abandoning me. That is what he wanted to speak about today.* Gisela's rational mind popped up. *How can you know? This is impossible. It is wishful thinking, not the truth. He is a self-serving aristocrat.* However, as she looked into the molten honey gaze of the man she loved, she knew beyond any doubt, he loved her and wished to marry her.

Gisela returned her attention to Hilarion. He wore his righteous envy like a black cloak about him. It oozed hatefulness. She knew there was nothing she could say. He believed what he said and not even the absolute truth could alter his path. *As always, Hilarion is walking the path of his own misconceptions and cares nothing for the feelings of others or the truth underlying the snippets he knows. He bends the world to his belief. All else is irrelevant.* Sadness welled within her. It was a deep, heart-wrenching ache that seared through her. Hilarion was beyond her reach. The gift she carried within her, the grace offered by the dragon lords who blessed her with life-giving fire, was meaningless before such blind hatred. Stale air burned in her lungs and she closed her eyes for the briefest of moments. A heavy sigh ached, and she grudgingly let it pass her lips.

Then her gaze fell on something her subconscious mind had been screaming about ever since Hilarion had made his appearance. How could she have missed this detail? Her mind was filled with the sight of the cloak he held draped over his arm. The dark outer material was mostly concealed. All she saw was the deep violet lining, shimmering silk. Purple. Royal purple. The shade so expensive it was exclusive to the wealthiest among the wealthy—and reserved, by default, to the royal family.

The thought dropped into an impressionist pool of abstract images. Once the ripples subsided, Gisela was presented a crystal clear picture—sharp and in focus. Everything fit exquisitely. All the little nagging worries that had tugged at her subconscious mind since she met the stranger, this man she knew as Albert, all of them fell into their rightful places to present a complete image. The softness she noticed, the lack of chiselled lines she was so familiar with the hard-working men around her, made sense with the thought of a man who exercised but did not labour. The smooth touch of his gentle fingers, more familiar with holding a pen than callous-engendering farm-tools.

Albert. It hit her like a sack of river sand. *The older brother who died.* In the flash of recognition, she understood his hesitation when she had used that name. She recalled the twitch of his brows and how he drew away from her as she breathed *Albert*, during their passionate embrace. *Albert is the dead older brother,* she realised. His words about his bereaved parents hurtled through her mind as she found his honey-coloured eyes. *Vincent. Crown prince. Heir to the realm.* No wonder he'd kept his identity secret. No wonder he'd struggled so when he wanted to tell her the truth.

Gisela found her hand clutching at her heart as though she could stop the shattering that would tear her into a million shards. The pain was unbearable. All she wanted was to close her eyes and blot out the clarity brought on by knowledge, but she was transfixed. *I cannot marry him*, the next thought struck her. Lightning frazzling her already shredded nerves. *I'm no queen. I'm a simple country girl. It is impossible.* Her chest heaved, she strained as panic engulfed her. *Today is proof enough that I'm not meant for this.* Hilarion's judgement echoed in her mind: *You are no queen, and you have no right to represent Ylvaton. And I have no right to usurp Vendale either*, her own harsh voice added. *This is just a taste of what will befall me in the next tier if I try to reach so high. I will only fall lower.*

She shook her head. It was impossible. *No matter how much Alber—no Vincent—wants to make me his wife, it cannot be. I'll bring ruin to the kingdom. I'm nothing—no one.* White-light panic tore through her. Gisela started losing sense of her surroundings. What should she do? What *could* she do? Vincent was out of her reach. That much was certain. Her gaze broke his at long last and flickered back to Hilarion, but she hastily retreated. *No, I've been through this. It isn't an option either. I cannot marry a man I do not love. Especially now, after this. We will only bring misfortune on each other.*

Her eyes darted, searching out the only other man she had ever turned to. In the sea of faces looking up at her, expectant, she picked out the stern, square jaw of her father. His eyes popped out of his skull, a mirror of a previous night that now foreshadowed this one. His face was a mask of shock and she even detected the bitterness of disappointment in the depths of his dark brown eyes. They were hard, unmoving. Her mind called up his ferocious contempt for dancers: *Dancers are shameful women who bring dishonour on their families. Dancing is a sin against the greatness of the gods. It is a disgrace, a dishonourable abasement.*

While her eyes locked with those of her father, Gisela was dragged into a maelstrom of wheeling images. Her perspective deepened as though she were being dragged through time. She spun through the kaleidoscope, catching flashes here and glimpses there. In a split second, she envisioned a life being shunned by her father whom she had dishonoured and who had been faced with ridicule from her suitors. He would not forgive her. She would endure months of silent brooding from her progenitor, and then, more final rejection with banishment from her home. She would find refuge in the mountains, living a life of asceticism. A life of loneliness, lovelessness and childlessness. The weight of such a life bore down on her.

Just as suddenly, she stood reeling at the top of the stage on harvest festival night. The moon illuminated her with its gentle light and the stars dazzled the darkened sky. She blinked. The future was clear. There was no place for her in her father's home either. She had nowhere to go. None of the men in her life could offer her a safe haven, and she knew her entire society would shun her. Gisela realised her purpose as a messenger of the gods was also completely thwarted by this one event. The message she had been given fell on deaf ears now. *There is nothing left for me. Hilarion outdid himself. Nothing remains. My life, it is over.*

At last, another detail impressed itself on her. She became aware of the object Hilarion held in his other hand. She noted the detail on the hilt of the sword he carried. A rampant white stag gleamed in the moonlight, a golden crown encircling the ball of the hilt between the creature's antlers. Yet another confirmation of her lover's true identity. *How can Hilarion be so blind?* She wondered. He hasn't managed to piece together that it is no mere lord he confronts, but the crown prince. She almost laughed at the innocence Hilarion demonstrated, but once more the sand dunes on her tongue parched any sound before it could escape her.

The sword drew her further. An idea struck—that resounding knell of ruin. Gisela hesitated. Her eyes dashed from Hilarion, to Vincent, to her father. Then, in one decisive motion, she made her decision. She strode forward. Crimson skirts billowed up, portend of what was to come. She raised her hands. One clasped around the cool, hard surface of the sword hilt while the other careened into Hilarion's chest, sending him tumbling backwards, down the stairs and into Vincent, who still stood transfixed. While the two men collapsed in a crumpled heap, Gisela turned the short blade in one swift motion and plunged the sharp steel into her abdomen and then upward as far as she could.

Pain seared white hot from the smithy's forge. Her legs gave way and her fingers numbed at the intensity of the injury. A dull throb replaced the initial incandescence. With each pulsating heartbeat, Gisela's skirts took on a more vibrant crimson than their original dye had ever bestowed. Red. The colour of life. The shade of the flame she had been when she brought her divine gift to her community. Now it was also the shade she saw as she drifted. *Always was my favourite colour*, she mused. *Oh gods. There's so much of it.*

Gisela's vision blurred. She heard a tumult, a clamouring, but the sounds washed over her—a gentle breeze, nothing more. The stars pulsated, gleaming brighter. She swam in a lake of glowing embers. Another agonizing stab seared through her, consuming every fibre in her body. The silvery stars streaked in an arc. She was vaguely aware of hard floorboards pressing into her hip. A rocking motion trickled into her awareness, but a heavy fog enveloped her mind and did not allow her to focus on the movement or what it meant.

One thing did draw her out of the muggy realm of pain and death. She heard a harrowing bellow echoing through the night sky. She knew that voice. The distress she heard in it pulled her back into the cacophony of screeching, wailing voices and distressed faces. Her father's grief-stricken visage tore into view. Loss clawed over his features, tearing at her heart as well. *Selfish,* she thought. *Rash. Unthinking.* With a final effort, she broke through the silence. "I'm sorry, Da," she murmured, a sparkling tear making its slow journey down her cheek, before the soft radiance took her into the overwhelming embrace of oblivion.

~

Vincent felt himself fall. His hip bumped into the ground, jarring against the hard, uneven surface, but he was oblivious to the physical pain. His eyes could not tear away from Gisela as she wielded the sword. He watched in painstaking slowness as his own blade arced, gleaming shimmering silver in the moonlight, and then tore crimson shreds into the body he held so dear.

He flung Hilarion's stocky weight off him, flew to his feet and fought his way to her side, stumbling on the stairs, but not allowing the blunder to pull him off balance. He threw himself onto his knees, skidding to a halt beside her crumpled form. He pulled her onto his lap, cradling her head against him.

"No, no, no!" he uttered, as though his negation could undo what unfolded in his arms. *Gods. So much blood.* The slick substance gushed everywhere, turning his whole world red.

His vision blurred, but he hardly felt the glistening

tears streak their way to his chin. The droplets burned, but it was nothing compared to the experience of his shattering heart. Life lost all meaning as he watched his beloved seep out of existence. His hands desperately tried to staunch the flow, but her heart kept pumping it out of the jagged wound in her belly.

"Nooooooo!" Vincent heard his own adamant negation echoed back at him in an ear-shattering bellow. He saw Gisela's eyes flare wide and lock onto the source of the sound. He glanced up to see the grief-stricken face of a father losing his only daughter streaking into view. Vincent's heart froze. Unbearable pain seared through him with the loss he heard and saw from the man he had judged so harshly a few days before.

"I'm sorry, Da," her melodious voice whispered in the last moment before she was pulled from Vincent's embrace and clutched in the possessive grasp of her devastated father. Dry sobs racked through the man who screamed wordlessly into the night sky. Vincent sat while the cool breeze played about him, his own grief overwhelmed by the inconsolable man beside him. Everything faded to sterile white, where numbness took over. All thoughts, all emotions, all perceptions were drowned out in the destruction wreaked by one desperate girl.

~

Mr Winry had met her steady gaze with fury blazing in his heart. What had Hilarion said? *Skank... intimately acquainted... give herself... whore... How could she?* Fiery-orange brimstone-bubbles rose in his chest. He felt the eyes of the crowd boring into him. *Just as expected,* he imagined the townsfolk saying. *Trust the Winry family to bring shame to the town. What a disgrace.* The bubbles burst incandescent liquid that seared his insides. *How could she?*

What happened then, came so fast his mind could not grasp it. The next thing he knew, his daughter knelt on the stage with her lifeblood pouring from her. Proud Farmer Winry launched himself through the crowd before his mind even knew what his body was doing. A roar tore through his chest as his memory superimposed another, long-suppressed image over the scene before him. His recollections presented him with his younger sister's broken body, smashed to pieces on the mountainside after she threw herself off a cliff. The details were fresh, as though he'd found her in that moment. Her distended belly, which she'd dutifully hidden for weeks at home, was visible for all to see. He never did find out who got her with child and then allowed her to bring her own death and that of the unborn child.

His knees landed hard on the solid floorboards of the stage, wiping away the sickening memory of his sister's shattered skull. All he was left with was the self-mutilated body of his daughter. Her head rolled loosely as he gathered her into his arms. Desolation tore through his soul in an upheaval of immense proportions. From one moment to the next, his heart went from a living, if overgrown, garden, to a barren wasteland where nothing would grow in the sun-baked dirt.

A father howled his pain at the moon, screamed his loss into the star-spangled sky. He found no consolation in the tranquil beauty his dragon gods bestowed. Everything was as dust before the enormity of his bereavement. *Why?* Was all his spent mind could formulate in accusation. He screamed and riled until all that was left was a spent shell, a hollow vessel where once a man had stood.

~

Hilarion watched the disintegration in disbelief. His mind struggled to make head or tail of the situation. *What?* He kept thinking over and over again, but kept coming up blank. His memory replayed Gisela's response, the way she shoved him away from her with force and determination beyond his imagining. His wide eyes watched repeatedly as she plunged the deadly weapon into her belly, and he relived the spurt of crimson that followed. *This isn't what I wanted.*

The winged reptile which had taken up residence in his chest cavity and had honed his revengeful exertions had been expelled with Gisela's forceful shove. Hilarion was left with a shrivelled excuse for a heart. It would not beat. It ached and sent spasms through his limbs. Blood poured from Gisela copiously, while his own oozed in a sluggish, congealing flow making movement impossible and thought meaningless.

Mr Winry's bellow tore through Hilarion's eardrum

bringing the scene on the stage into sharp focus. The other dancers had fled, leaving Gisela clutched to her father's chest and her lover collapsed beside them. The two men next to her limp form radiated loss and anguish. A series of disjointed thoughts trickled through the sieve of Hilarion's mind until they condensed into something he could grasp. *What have I done?* Self-blame and guilt constricted what remained of his heart until spots appeared in his vision. The strength of his emotions erased all perceptions. Darkness, more solid and unyielding than his own jealousy, enveloped him. Silence wiped all the clamouring spectators out of existence. An unyielding pain consumed his sense of touch. *What have I done?*

Gisela's lifeless form swam into view, and promptly, his sight shut down again, refusing to acknowledge the harrowing reality his mindless jealousy created. The burden of his guilt grew larger with every passing breath, and at long last, Hilarion did what he always did. He fled. His feet carried him through the night, far from prying eyes and accusing voices, but he could not escape self-recrimination and the weight of his thoughtless actions. The light in his life, the flame that had kindled his spirit, was snuffed out, and it was entirely his fault.

PART II

SHATTERED DREAMS

32

Vincent was furious. He paced back and forth on the upper floor of the inn. Lava burned through his veins and flambéed his innards. He seethed. With fists clenched, he turned his irate thoughts to the priest. *How dare he? That pompous, inconsiderate, fool!*

The priest's words echoed in Vincent's mind. *It is impossible. She is officially unvirtuous and took her own life. She cannot be laid in consecrated ground. I cannot allow such a disgrace. The sacred dragons would curse us all for disregarding their holy principles.*

Vincent spun around and marched back across the room. He kept his fists clenched to control the urge to fling things about him. More than anything, he wanted to vent his anger on the objects in reach, but he set his jaw as he overpowered the thoughts by turning his attention to the memory of Gisela's mother pleading for clemency while her father stood by in a speechless daze. "And they wouldn't even listen to me," he muttered under his breath. "No one cared that her virtue actually remained intact." After a momentary pause, Vincent cried out, "Curse that mistaken fool of a gamekeeper and his jealous mind."

In mid-stride, his legs gave way beneath him. Vincent sank to his knees, his fists resting against the rough wooden floor. *Curse him. Curse him!* Glittering droplets forced their way out into the open and rolled down Vincent's cheeks. He crumpled forward, his head hitting the floor with a soft thunk, and then a wordless howl spilled forth. Vincent's body rocked while his head remained plastered to the floorboards. Pent up anger, frustration and the agony of his loss tore through him and froze all who were assembled on the lower floor of the inn.

The storm of misery passed, and silence filled the inn once more. Vincent remained prostrated. Getting up cost too much effort. He was spent. The emotional turmoil left behind a fuzzy greyness. His energy leaked into the air around him, sapping his will to do anything that day. He remained that way for a time, wondering what he could do to help Gisela's parents with a burial place. He couldn't force the priest's hand without fully giving away his identity. He wanted to avoid that scenario if possible. *What can I do? Where can she be laid to rest?*

A sudden flash of inspiration sent blinding white

lightning crackling through him. He stood in one fluid motion. *I can help.*

The instant the thought coursed through him, he knew how he could support the Winry family in this matter of Gisela's burial. He was already half-way down the stairs when he called for his close companions to follow him. He hastened towards the festival grounds where Gisela's body was laid out for the wake. The sky was grey, a perfect match for the colourlessness in his soul. It harmonised well with his sense of loss, and he was grateful for the absence of the sun. Sunlight would be unbearable in the void she left behind.

Vincent marched into the tent, ignoring the few villagers who stood outside, craning their necks and whispering to each other with knowing looks. He stopped in his tracks at the sight before him. Gisela's body lay on a table in the centre of the tent. She was dressed in the grey dress she'd worn for their tryst, but this time there was no green shawl to add colour to his world. Her mother sat on a stool against one tent wall. The younger of her two sons leaned over her, his hand rubbing her hunched back while he whispered consoling words. She answered only with sobs and long, silent cries. Gisela's father sat crumpled in the farthest corner. He said nothing, only stared ahead. Eyes wide but unseeing, Farmer Winry remained paralysed in his place.

The older brother stood to one side, and Vincent

stepped towards him. Although he addressed the room at large, Vincent looked to the other man, who was his own age and a little taller than he. "I would like to offer you the opportunity of interring Gisela in the forest. You can choose a place near your farm. I know she loved the forest, and it is a peaceful place for her final rest."

Sven Winry said, his voice acidic, "Bringing about this calamity isn't enough for you? You want us all to be killed for trespassing on the king's land like that?"

Vincent waved away the accusation and retorted, "I'll handle the king. You needn't fear that. I shall personally ensure you get dispensation, and nothing will happen. Besides, I am the highest authority in this town at the moment. I don't see any impediment. She needs a resting place, and if the church won't honour a woman who clearly was sufficient in virtue to become a message of life and growth from the gods, then I'll do my part to ensure she is treated with honour and dignity."

The two men locked gazes for a moment. Sven lowered his eyes first and mumbled, "As you wish, my lord." He stepped back and turned to his mother and brother. They were oblivious to the exchange. Sven squared his shoulders then and said, "There is a clearing near our house. She often went there. I suppose it is as good a place as any."

"Then we are agreed," Vincent answered. "Tell my

men when you wish to begin, and I shall send some ahead to dig the grave."

Sven shook his head. His dark curls bounced about his face. "No, sir. That, Robert and I will do. I expect we'll do so right away."

33

Hilarion sat on a log, cradling his head in his hands. The breeze rustled in the leaves, a thousand voices to reconfirm the recriminations piercing his core. Grey clouds flowed overhead and, on occasion, rays of sunlight filtered into the clearing where he perched. His mind was an ocean. Waves crashed onto infertile rocks sending spray flying and leaving the taste of salt.

Wailing voices drew his attention to a procession that approached him. Through the trees, he saw two tall figures walking along the path, bearing a single item on their shoulders. Behind them followed a number of people. Hilarion realised they were coming his way and, embarrassed about the tears he'd spilled, he took three quick steps and disappeared behind a nearby beech tree. Flakes of copper drifted down from the branches above him and settled on the ground at his feet—the tree weeping blood for the one being borne into the clearing.

Sven and his brother Robert came into view, and Hilarion saw they were bearing a pale poplar casket. Searing pain tore through his chest. It felt like he'd drunk sea water. He pressed himself into the tree trunk and observed farmer Winry and his wife hobbling into view. Their heads were bowed and Gisela's mother wailed in her grief while the man beside her walked as though in a trance. His soul was absent, and the realisation sent a shudder through Hilarion.

Then his attention was drawn away by movement behind the Winrys. Eyes narrowed, he watched the aristocrat, his head uncharacteristically bowed forward with eyes on the ground, shuffle into the open space between the forest vegetation. *Accursed man,* Hilarion's fists clenched and the muscles in his jaw bulged as he bit down hard, teeth grinding with a crunch. *Selfish, unthinking agent of this...world where she is gone.*

The pallbearers lowered the coffin on the side of the clearing opposite Hilarion's hiding place. Gisela's brothers then set about digging. They were powerful young men and the ground was soft. Their motions were quick and smooth. The monotony of this physical labour dulled the loss and pain which hung over the small gathering that waited.

Hilarion studied his rival. The lord hung back. He gave the Winry family space and stayed in the company of two other men. One, Hilarion recognised as the companion who accompanied the lord on most of his outings, and the second was the muscular man he'd identified as the lord's bodyguard. Hilarion shifted and scowled at the group of three, throwing silent epithets at them.

It did not take long for a sizeable hole to materialise in the clearing. The Winry brothers stepped back and grounded their spades next to the mound of dark earth they had excavated. Sven wiped a hand over his brow while Robert pulled out a large, blue handkerchief he used to pat his face dry. Sven plucked the fabric from his brother's hands before Robert could stow it in his pocket.

The group huddled closer to the wooden casket, and Hilarion heard the aristocrat murmur for a few minutes. He could not make out the words, but understood it was the lord who spoke over Gisela before she would be lowered into the ground. *Why are they burying her here?* His veins iced over when the answer hit him. *The church wouldn't have her.* He reeled in the tempest of such injustice. *After all her dedication. With her unwavering belief and everything she did to serve, they would not allow her to rest in her sanctuary.* His frown deepened into a ravine. *I always told her the church was a place of men, and she'd not find the gods there.* And now she would rest in his forest forever because of the wiles of humans.

Hilarion watched the wooden rectangle being lowered into shadowy depths and out of sight. A series of images played across his memory. Gisela laughing, her eyes closed, and her joy rippling out of her with all the abandon of her zest for life. It was followed by her pout with the little crevice that formed between her eyebrows as they arched over her intense gaze. Next, the way she tugged at a braid when she was nervous or anxious. The way she held her head high and looked out with wholehearted fulfilment when she danced. How she gazed through people and into their inner selves to find what was best in them.

Glittering tears streamed down his cheeks, unheeded. He turned away from the group of people in the clearing. Gisela was gone. The ache consuming his whole being was more than he could bear. He pressed his knuckles against his teeth, stifling a howl as it built in his chest. His teeth pressing into the skin against the bones of his hands brought relief from the overwhelming emotional cesspit that was his being. *Why me?* His mind screeched with numbing intensity. *What have I ever done to deserve all this pain?*

Not wanting to draw attention to his presence, he bent his knees and hunched over them, his hands clutching the rough, dirt-spattered fabric of his trouser legs. He rested his head on his knees and fought the ever-increasing stream of tears. *Why does everyone always leave me?* He bit down hard on his knee, shutting off the scream that wanted to burst forth. *Why does this always happen to me? Why?*

After a lengthy period, Hilarion noticed that

Gisela's family, and the lord with his entourage, were leaving. Their movement, and the changed weight of the air around him, pulled Hilarion out of his misery and allowed the river from his soul to pause its flowing. He waited and listened to their retreating footsteps along the well-trodden path. The sun hung low in the sky, falling beneath the grey blanket shielding it all day. The forest blazed in the sun's glory, the trees a colour-reflection of that fiery source of all life.

Once birds returned to the clearing, chirping their excited songs and settling in the branches overhead in preparation for the coming night, Hilarion stepped away from his hiding place. He walked out into the light. It blazed onto his cheek, blinding him. While he blinked the brightness away with his darkness, Hilarion took another step. The scent of earth invaded his nose. He saw a mound of dark earth, still damp from its recent rest underground. It was all that remained of the woman he'd once loved.

He stopped. *No headstone*, he thought. A stillness spread inside him. *This is not right*. The conviction was overwhelming. *I must do something.* He looked around. A large log lay to one side of the grave. His memory tugged him into an image of Gisela sitting on that broken tree less than a year before, when the barren winter gave way to the green shoots of spring. She had leaned in to receive the sunlight that streamed into the clearing with soft warmth. He shook his head. *No time for that*. Hilarion searched for something he could use, not another pointless memory of the woman who lay beneath the ground in that clearing.

A large stone caught his eye. It lay among the roots of a sturdy oak tree. Hilarion brushed earth away from the edges of the rock and heaved. It came away from its resting place easily, and he noted its egg shape. *Perfect*, he mused. *This will do nicely.* It did not take him long to arrange it at the head of the fresh grave. He stepped back, hands on his hips. His lips twitched upward only to fall again. He turned away. In three brisk strides, he returned to the beech tree where he'd found shelter earlier in the day. He jumped and pulled a branch low. Then he snapped some twigs from it with his other hand. His face turned serious while he wove the swatches of leafy crimson into a wreath.

Returning to the grave, Hilarion placed the wreath on Gisela's tombstone. He did not even realise his choice reflected the shade of the creature Gisela had manifested the evening before. He'd been too blinded by hate and jealousy to observe the miracle of the Harvest Queen. Now, he felt content with his efforts and knelt before the grave.

In the silence, a small voice echoed, *Does it have to be about you? This happened. It is not about you.* He opened his eyes wide and bit his lip. He tried to resist the voice, to push it from him, but it continued, persistent. *Your parents were ill. Sickness happens in all families. It was never about you. You chose to dwell in death instead of living life.*

Eyes widening in understanding, Hilarion's tears spilled. He wept in earnest. For himself. For his blindness. For Gisela and her unpredictable decision, and for the life he believed she should have lived. Silver drops fell for his family and all the years he'd rejected and renounced the world—for all the years of his life he'd allowed to stream by without living. Spent at last, Hilarion allowed silence to fill him. He knelt in the dirt and watched the sunlight fade into starlight. The night sounds of the peaceful forest washed over him, healing the dark rift he'd nurtured for many long years. Tranquillity provided its mantle at long last and Hilarion's lips twitched into a true smile, deeply serene, in over a decade.

Hilarion sat up with a start. He blinked and rubbed his knuckles into his eye-sockets. *Must have fallen asleep*, he mused. He shivered. The air was cool. The moon's disk hung high in the sky. He shivered again. He saw mist gathering. There was something eerie about how it moved in grasping wisps. The leaves rustled overhead. He felt the next ripple go up his spine when he noticed a silent, translucent, shimmering figure float into the clearing.

Scrambling backwards on hands and feet, Hilarion gasped when more figures bobbed into view. All were women, their misty skirts swaying on the air. Eyes wide with terror, Hilarion didn't feel the rock he'd placed at the head of Gisela's grave press into his spine. All his attention was drawn to the host of glowing shadows circling him. Their voices rasped like the crackle of leaves in a gale.

Sister, they murmured. *It is time to rise.*

Iciness spread crystalline facets through Hilarion's veins. The hairs on the back of his neck stood on end and he watched a presence materialise from the grave beneath his feet. The rock at his back stopped him from being able to retreat any further, but it did not stop his legs from flailing in desperation. He was struck dumb. His brain transformed into soup while he watched the misty figure take on the familiar form of his beloved Gisela.

Flakes, white as snow, formed on his lower lip, searing into the dry surface. A glacial drought tore through his throat, stifling the scream that wanted to burst forth from his chest. Eyes circled white, he stared at the apparition, a luminescent wisp of misty light with an orange tinge to it. Skirts swayed in a non-existent wind. Two long braids swung softly. She raised a hand, stretched out to him, and he shrank back even further. It was her eyes that terrified him most; they were sheer, obsidian pools.

The silence of death was broken by Gisela's soft, sighing voice. "Hilarion. It was never about you. You always chose to take things personally." Her tone was gentle, but there was a firmness to it he'd never heard before. “When I saw that I could not become Vincent’s wife because I am not suitable for that station, and I believed my father would never forgive me, I chose a path. That decision had nothing to do with you and most certainly wasn’t envisioned as abandoning you. I simply never loved you, and perhaps that is because you wished to use me as a cheerful dressing for the wounds of your soul. The thing is, you would have drained me of all my happiness. I rejected you instinctively, and it was cruel, but now I understand why it was so. I could not be your wife because you never loved me for my own sake. You only ever loved me for your sake and how you felt in my presence.”

Hilarion quivered in his prostrate position. Unable to break the intensity of her gaze, he stared back with his face contorted into a mask of fear. She shook her head, her braids weaving around her. “You don’t need to fear me, Hilarion. I don’t begrudge you what has happened. It was my choice, and I stand by it. I bear you no ill-will and have no intention of harming you.”

“How can you say that?” one of the other ghosts snapped, her voice crackling static. “He is the cause of your death.” The figure stepped forward. She was tall and elegant with high cheekbones, although her bluish luminescence was thinner, more stretched, than most of the other spirits. She, too, had two braids and wore a dress of a different style from Gisela’s. Hilarion wondered how long this ghost had roamed the forests.

An unknown power surged within Hilarion. He

had a confession to make. "Gisela," he whispered. "I cursed you, that day. After you refused me. I cursed you, and whatever gods or demons were there, listened. I didn't want this. I didn't mean it, not really."

"You see!" exclaimed the haughty phantom. "He freely admits his own guilt!" Then she turned and addressed Hilarion in a sing-song voice. "And you learned the lesson, though too late: be careful what you wish for!"

Gisela turned to the other spectre. "He is not at fault," she maintained in a strong and silky spider-thread voice. "Hilarion was hurt and did what he deemed right from the warped nature of his heart. I did not go after him to clarify the situation, although I was certain it was he who saw me with Vincent. I knew there was a risk he might misunderstand what he saw, but I lacked the courage to confront him about it. It was also I who committed the violence to my own body. Hilarion did nothing to harm me. I harmed myself and am entirely responsible for my actions."

A ripple of belligerent laughter echoed through the clearing. The same haughty ghost added, "You would defend him after everything he's done to you? She doesn't get it, does she?" The leader addressed the remainder of the assembly. More laughter filtered from the host of ghosts. The lead spirit's gaze darkened to determination. "Well, let's see how defensible he is. Come, we are gathered here to dance, let's see if he is man enough and innocent enough to dance with us, sisters!"

Gisela shifted, placing herself between the other ghost and Hilarion, but the older spectre only smiled. It was a wicked grin that spoke of a hunger for revenge so large it would never be satiated. She leaned over Gisela's shoulder, leered at Hilarion and then turned in a swift motion as though blown by a gust of wind. He observed the host of spirits swaying. He felt a tension rise in his chest. The whole forest seemed to thrum at a vibration that shook him to the core of his being. The ghosts began to dance in silence, their spectral forms lit from within and from the light of the moon which hung suspended in a starless sky. Goosebumps prickled over his skin. He watched the souls of all these women dance and weave about in time to some unheard music. They whirled and floated in a choreographed sea of motion. Their wispy mist-forms dispersed with the movements and then re-gathered themselves.

Hilarion noticed how beautiful they all were. The cold gripping his body began to release its hold over him, and he watched in awe as the maidens danced. There were so many of them and, yet, each one was breathtakingly beautiful in her own right. He released his clenching hold on the rock and shifted to get a better view.

Gisela turned her vaporous face towards him and said, "Stay here, on my grave. They cannot harm you here where you are. They cannot reach you. Know, that should they lure you, you will be lost."

Hilarion swallowed hard and nodded. He continued to watch the dancing and after a while noticed Gisela among them. Her movements were even more magical than he remembered and he settled more comfortably to watch. *Such alluring women*, he thought. *Enchanting.* When one of them glided past him and beckoned, he did not draw back. *Charming,* his mind offered, but he stayed where he was.

Another ghost sidled up to him and blew him a languorous kiss. His breath hitched in his throat as he watched the spirit swaying her well-defined hips as she moved. When she glanced over her shoulder, Hilarion stood. The power of his attraction to this creature of light and fog overwhelmed him. In a trance, he stumbled after the ghost. Moments later, one of the spirits grasped him by the arms. He looked down at where the freezing sensation knifed into him, just below his elbows, but his strength of will was no match for the power of the spectre. The presence pulled his eyes to gaze into the deep black pools, and he realised it was the one who'd spoken to Gisela before. He noticed she wore a crown of birch twigs which shimmered silver in the moonlight.

"If the new one won't have her revenge," the ghost whispered, "then I, at least, can have some sport. Come, dance with me. Join me in my revels."

Hilarion allowed himself to be swept away. Numbness spread through him, and he struggled to keep pace. Still, he could not tear his gaze from the beauty who ensnared him. He didn't hear Gisela's dismayed shriek. He didn't even notice a chain of the other dancers form around Gisela to keep her away from him and the ghost who danced with him. He leapt and galloped in the arms of his partner, ignoring the stabs of pain that gouged through his chest with every breath.

Oblivious to the passage of time or the route they took, he kept dancing. His feet moved without his brain's assistance. As the minutes passed, his motions became more and more disjointed. His head jerked and then his foot trod on a loose stone. Stumbling to the ground, Hilarion grazed his knee, but pushed himself back up with force.

A different spirit woman drew him to her. This one had a round face and full lips. He grinned in response to her coy smile. His brain had long since ceased firing any thoughts. It was suspended, blanketed by fog in female form that surrounded him.

He didn't notice the terrain rising or the trees thinning. He was passed from one gorgeous woman to another until solid ground disappeared underfoot. The spirits continued floating in the moonlit air, laughing and singing, while a heavy body plummeted down a steep ravine and came to a sudden, crunching stop.

In the town, a few miles away, the church bell rang out a single, prolonged note. A collective sigh rose up in the forest and mountains. Luminescent shapes drifted back into fog, covering the ground with a cotton-wool blanket. The forest returned to its night-time sounds; some frogs croaked in a nearby pond, nocturnal creatures rustled through their nightly activities. Serenity spread throughout the lower slopes, and only the crows paid heed to the body they found a short while after dawn, once the sun climbed above the craggy peaks and bathed the valley in gold.

34

Vincent woke at dawn with a chill shiver. He sat up, startled by something in his dream. In the fleeting moment between sleep and waking, the images of his vision slipped the grasp of his mind. Shaking his head, he lay back again. Sleep overtook him once more, and he woke hours later with no memory of his startle at sunrise.

During the day, he struggled with indecision. *I should do it*, he thought. He'd square his shoulders, take a few steps, and then another consideration flashed through his mind. *It would be odd. They'd probably take it the wrong way.* Shoulders falling forward, Vincent headed back the way he'd come. *But they will need the support. It is the least I can do,* he countered. *It's so awkward. Better not put myself in such a position. What is done is done and that's that.*

That is heartless. They just lost their daughter.

Doing it will just make them believe more firmly that the gamekeeper's accusations are true. How does that help their memory of her?

But it is the right thing to do.

Sometimes what is right is callous. Better to keep her memory as unspoilt as possible.

It's already tainted beyond all proportion. At least this could do some good.

What about the festival this evening? Isn't that continuing? Wouldn't it be best to make an appearance?

That's not important. What's important is the Winry family and their future.

He argued back and forth with himself for several hours. Oskar checked in a few times, but hesitated on the threshold. Vincent noticed his friend but ignored him. *I don't want to talk to him. He'd just make fun of her, call it an adventure and then ask when we're heading back. I don't want to go home,* he affirmed, clutching the armrest of a chair. *I cannot go backwards, and I don't want to go forwards. What to do?*

At least make things right, or as right as they'll ever be after this, with her family. They need it.

So it continued for many hours more. The sun hung low in the sky when he pulled himself together, pushed all counter arguments aside with a firm *I have decided,* and strode out the inn without a backward glance. After a brisk walk, Vincent reached the Winry family's farmhouse. The log building stood sturdy and warm in the late-afternoon light. All was calm. He saw one of the young men herding the sheep into the barn. The sound of bleating brought a smile to his lips. He took a deep breath, absorbing the wholesome smells of the earth and the farm. The mountains raised their majestic peaks into an azure sky. He marvelled at the intensity of the golden cloak, streaked with greens and reds, swaying from the shoulders of the mountains.

Gisela's mother sat in a rocking chair on the porch, enjoying the afternoon glow. Her knitting needles danced out a masterful pattern, swift and sure. Although she appeared calm, cloaked in tranquillity, Vincent sensed a deep sadness coming from her. He took another deep breath and approached her, his hands trembling. She looked up, nodded her head and returned her attention to the needles in her hand. Vincent glanced through the doorway as he stepped up onto the porch. A dishevelled figure sat by the large kitchen table, elbows resting on the surface and propping his head up with his hands. Matted hair stood up on end and Vincent noticed, his eyebrows flying up as he did so, that Mr Winry still wore the same clothes he'd had on the evening of the harvest festival.

Turning to the woman with greying hair sparkling in the low sunlight, Vincent nodded his head while inwardly reaffirming his determination. *More than I even imagined, they need help.* Then, he stepped forward and addressed the woman in her rocking chair. "Mrs Winry, I would like to support your family in this difficult time." Her eyes locked onto his. There was so much of Gisela in that gaze. His heart stopped for a second. His voice died in the back of his throat, and he cleared it twice. "I would like to give you this." He fumbled with a knotted tie on his belt. When it came free, he cupped a small leather pouch in his hand and handed it to Mrs Winry.

A sharp, angry voice cut in from behind Vincent. "You think you can pay us off for the harm you've caused?" Vincent spun around to face Robert. "Money can't bring her back! She's gone and it's your fault! You cannot buy our silence. And you can't allay your conscience with a few pennies. We don't want your money."

Eyes wide, Vincent protested, "No... no. That's not my intention. I wanted..." He trailed off. The animosity billowing off the proud young man intimidated Vincent more than his own father ever had. *I am doing what is right. I will not back off*, the thought pierced through Vincent's dithering indecision. Taking a calming breath, Vincent squared his shoulders and turned to face Robert's wrath head on. "I had every intention of marrying Gisela," he said. His voice exuded calm decision, and Vincent rejoiced at the firmness and strength it gained. "I don't know why she did what she did, but I don't see why your family shouldn't receive something to help you through troubling times. You are now in even greater need than ever of the money I would have paid as her dowry. Your father is ill. My mother was like that," he gestured to the figure huddled within, "for years after my brother died. That could be the end of this farm. I don't want your livelihood to suffer while your father fights his demons. It can take weeks or years, but from the way he looks, and the fact he hasn't even changed clothes since that night, I know he's in a bad way. I don't want to see your family suffer any more than you already are. Her passing is enough to bear." Vincent's voice hitched, but he saw Robert's face soften. The young man's composure revealed cracks of vulnerability. Loss and pain simmered in the well-pools of his eyes.

There was a creak of wooden floorboards and a rustle from behind Vincent. He turned to see Mrs Winry crossing the distance between them with two shuffling steps. She pulled him into her arms and although the crown of her head only came up to his chest, he felt safe. Her embrace enveloped him in the comfort of a warm blanket to ward off the icy winds of loss.

When she released him, Mrs Winry gazed up at him. "You are a good and kind man, my prince. I know you will make for a righteous king."

Vincent's eyes burned. He blinked back the tears pricking in his eyesockets.

"W—what?" Robert stammered behind them. Vincent half turned as the other young man continued in disbelief. "What madness is this, Mother? This man can't be the crown prince."

Although Vincent had never felt comfortable with his status, in that moment he felt like he wanted to deny it completely. Hanging his head and slumping his shoulders, he wanted to agree with Robert and disown himself, but he knew he could not. Somehow, before these humble, hard-working people, his noble bloodline felt dirty.

Before Vincent could say anything, Mrs Winry's stern voice changed the energy once more. "It baffles me how blind you can be. If you were to pay attention, Robert, His Highness' status would have been clear to you days ago."

Robert's eyes popped, and a gurgling sound came out of his open mouth. Mrs Winry continued speaking directly to her son's disbelief. "A grey cloak with purple lining. A sword with the rampant white stag on the hilt and a golden crown on the pommel. A man who has the power and the right to choose the King's Forest as Gisela's final resting ground. Aged twenty-four." She was holding up four fingers, which she'd counted off as she spoke. Incredulity spread over her face as she shook her head. "I don't understand how you men don't look deeper than what you are presented with at face value. You look past the obvious because you've already told yourselves what you are willing to believe."

Then, she turned her attention back to Vincent and taking his hands in hers, she said, "I have always been good at reading people, and if there's anyone I know in this world, it is my own daughter. In that moment, when she looked at you, just before making her decision, I saw she knew too. She worked it out, and she loved you more for it, but she has often allowed her realism to hold back the truth. She didn't feel in that instant that she was worthy or ever could be. That was the funny thing about Gise: she had so much belief for everyone around her, but never really any for herself."

She paused a moment, brushing away a lone tear that streaked down her cheek. Then she met Vincent's gaze once more and stated with firm conviction, "I do not hold you to blame for what happened. You love and respect my daughter. I can see that. I've seen it in every action I've observed you making. You are a good man."

Tears spilled from him. He tried to rein in the torment of emotions and settled for only revealing his agony through sparkling rivulets. After taking several breaths to steady himself, he managed a heartfelt, "Thank you." The short, ample woman squeezed his hands and let go her hold of him. She turned and took a step towards the main door of the house, but Vincent stopped her. He still held the pouch, and now he reached out, proffering it, and pleaded, "Please. Please accept this."

Mrs Winry nodded, glanced up at him with a faint smile and grasped the pouch.

"Thank you," Vincent said and left. He glanced back once to see the mother enveloping her son in a warm hug.

Vincent allowed the breeze to refresh him. As the creeks his tears had streaked dried, the young prince felt his spirit renew. *It was the right thing, and who could have known her mother was so wonderful?* He reached the fork in the lane beside the Winry family's vineyard and was about to continue to Ylvaton when he stopped. *I should make my peace with her, too*, he thought and turned up the other path, heading in the direction of the forest.

He arrived at the clearing and took in the rough headstone and wilted wreath of flaming leaves. Footprints and other strange marks compacted some of the earthen mound which had been freshly turned the afternoon before. Vincent wondered whether this change was orchestrated by Hilarion. Then he shrugged and knelt before the grave to make his peace.

Hours passed and Vincent sat in peaceful tranquillity. He watched the sun set in a glorious display and for the first time in his life did not feel the need to move.

There was nothing pressing, and he had the time to just sit and bask in the grandeur of the world he lived in. The moon rose, no longer round and full, but marked by lopsidedness. He listened to the crickets chirping and the toads croaking in a nearby pond. Regular gusts of wind rustled a symphony among the leafy branches, and he smelled the intensity of the damp earth and forest around him.

The calm flowing through Vincent was unlike anything he'd ever experienced. He had this opportunity to just sit and be. It was a freedom he embraced with all his soul. He looked up to absorb the velvet darkness spangled with shimmering jewels far more beautiful than any he'd ever seen gracing a fine lady at his father's court. *Nature is grander and more magnificent than anything we humans can achieve.*

He sat as contentment ebbed and flowed in the grandeur of the ocean. The night deepened and still Vincent remained by Gisela's grave, basking in the silence. He knew the next day would bring upheaval. He pushed the knowledge of his imminent departure from his mind. No. He would allow himself this one night to keep the world at bay. *I am also important. My energy can go towards what I appreciate, too.*

The moon hung high overhead when Vincent heard the soft chiming of the church bell in Ylvaton. He started. *How strange that I can hear it at this distance,* he thought. *It's late.* The passing of time had caught him unawares. Vincent rose and stretched the stiffness from his muscles. A sudden thought flashed, *Oskar and Fred don't know where I am. I didn't tell them, and they must be worried. That was thoughtless of me. I should hurry to let them know all is well.*

Vincent stopped just as he took his first step away from the grave. A chill ran up his spine, raising the hairs on his neck and arms. He glanced about and saw tendrils of mist gathering around the clearing. Where had the mist come from? The timing for fog seemed off and it made his skin crawl to think that the unnatural was at work. His nerves tingled as his body went on high alert.

Moments later, the first translucent figure, skirts swaying in a non-existent wind, appeared at the edge of the clearing. He noticed the mist had already encircled him, and he backed up onto Gisela's grave, which he noted was the centre of the circle. More figures manifested. His heart pounded in his throat. He was cut off, with nowhere to run.

"Stay by me and all will be well," he heard Gisela's melodious voice echo through the unnatural stillness.

Her words were answered by a rising horde of cackles, but Vincent decided to trust her. He felt the other ghosts' belligerence and hoped Gisela could protect him. He edged closer to the headstone and glanced at the confident form swaying above Gisela's grave. She held her head higher, and there was a firmness to her gaze he did not recognise from before. Her kindness and compassion were still evident, despite the changes.

Looking upon the spectre of the woman he loved, Vincent felt his chest constrict. She seemed to sense his pain; her face contorted, and she floated closer. Her voice echoed in his head, *I won't allow any harm to come to you, my love. Please, stay where you are. Stay with me."*

The gathering of spirits crowded into the clearing, constricting the space and adding to Vincent's anxiety. One ghost came forward. She wore a simple peasant dress, much like Gisela's, but also different. The cut was from another time. Vincent saw a silvery birch crown gracing her blue-tinged filmy silhouette. Prominent cheekbones lent the spectre a haughty appearance. Her voice brought chills to his heart.

"Ah, another one. You have had good sport," she addressed Gisela. "I did not think we'd get to entertain another one so soon." A ripple of eerie laughter skittered through the crowd. Gisela drifted between the newcomer and Vincent. "You defend this one also?" The voice was sharp and scathing.

"Vincent is even less to blame for what happened than Hilarion was. He caused no deliberate harm."

"Nonsense!" came the disdainful reply. "He fed you lies and idle promises. You don't really believe any of the things he said to you. Certainly not now, when you know everything there is to know about him."

"You are wrong!" Gisela challenged. "This man is good. I watched him today. He went to support my parents because father is not himself. Mother even said he is good and kind, and I agree with her. She always knew how to read people, and I trust her judgement. You have no right to him. He is mine, and I will not relinquish him to you."

"Ha!" scoffed the other ghost. "You think he's loyal to you? That he truly loves you? Let's see if he's as faithful as that blockhead from last night." The thin ghost who appeared to be fraying at the edges swayed with a seductive motion in her hips and glanced towards Vincent before she launched into a vibrant dance.

The other spirits joined in. Soon they were swirling around the clearing—a cloud of the reanimated descended to the plane of the living. Vincent shivered. Gisela swayed in time to some unheard beat, but he was relieved she remained with him. Every now and then, one of the apparitions tried to approach him, but whirled away before reaching the grave. Vincent noticed their enticing glances and how they beckoned for him to follow. He shook his head every time and returned his gaze to Gisela, who fought the pull of whatever ghostly music they danced to.

Time passed, and he saw the gathering ghosts ripple in frustration. The lead wraith stopped before Gisela again, anger pouring from her. "Why do you defend him? He is but a man. They are all contemptible."

Gisela squared her shoulders and answered with uncharacteristic calm, "He is the best man I ever met. I do not hold him to blame for what happened. That is where you are wrong. You have dedicated aeons to your hate for his kind and never once took a moment to contemplate your own involvement in what happened. I was the only one to cause harm to myself. I did it, and I acknowledge my fault. No one else, not this man or any other had anything to do with my death. That was my choice. You choose to be the victim, but what will happen when you allow yourself the freedom of forgiveness?"

The adversary hissed and lunged forward, claws outstretched, willing to rake her filmy appendages over Vincent's face. A shockwave shook the air in the clearing and the hostile ghost was flung away from Vincent and Gisela. Eyes wide, showing the whites around the irises, Vincent stared first at the tossed figure and then at the web of golden strands encasing Gisela's grave like a dome of light. The ripple in the dome above stilled and it disappeared from view, dissolving into the air again.

"I won't let you have him," Gisela stated. "He must live, and I will see it done."

The animosity of the spectres grew. They hurled themselves at the protective sphere Gisela supported around her grave. Eventually the onslaught became too much for her, and she backed up, step after step, inching closer to Vincent. He observed the ghostly attack and how they maintained the dance even in their assault. Every movement was timed and choreographed to perfection.

When she could back no further, and her protective shield had shrunk to encompass only the headstone and Vincent beside her, the prince became aware of vast music. There was a chime to the leaves; the humming of woodwinds vibrated in the air; majestic strains echoed off the mountains. The whole landscape hummed to an epic concert that encompassed everything. He was drawn into the vastness and majesty of the natural world. He felt his own body respond at the same resonance and became aware of all living things harmonising in the music. *This is life—the resonance of creation. Almighty gods, it is beautiful!*

Awe turned to trepidation when Vincent saw Gisela's spirit begin to fade. She held on against the unceasing attack from the other spectres, but he saw her taking strain. The light, which in the beginning was a strong luminescence gleaming throughout her filmy form, was fading. The golden tendrils in the protective sphere above Vincent's head were becoming lethargic and glimmered with less intensity.

Fear gripped him. The night was still long. If she couldn't hold out against these fierce apparitions, how could he survive? He knew they held him responsible for something, but he didn't understand what it was. Gisela faded even more, and Vincent shut his eyes tight, reaching for the calm beyond his fear. Finding nothing but more intestine-gripping terror, he turned his thoughts to something he did believe in. *Oh, sacred dragon gods,* he prayed. *Please lend her strength that she might withstand this ordeal.*

The ringing pulsation along the protective barrier slowed its intensity. He opened his eyes and watched as the other ghosts, even more diaphanous than Gisela was in that moment, reined in their assault. Eyes wide, his breath coming short and fast, Vincent watched the spirits return to their original state. His heart calmed its panicked palpitations. He saw the figures, filled with vengeance only moments before, return to mist along the forest floor. Then, he watched as even that condensation dissipated.

Gisela held on longer than the others. She was right beside him, and he heard her whisper, "I'm so sorry, Vincent. I should have placed greater faith in us. In that moment, I felt like a hopeless failure; even the message the dragons sent through me fell on deaf ears. I couldn't see any way forward. My action was rash, and I see the pain I caused you. I'm sorry, my love."

Before he could respond, Vincent witnessed the glow within her snuff out. As it did, the visible form she'd taken on melted away. There was no return to the mist. She simply disappeared—ceased to exist. His soul cried out at the severance. This last, tiny part of the once vibrant woman slipped from his grasp and he knew with certainty she would never manifest in this world again.

Her grave felt empty. Earlier in the day, he had found comfort in this place. Now, it was void. There was nothing left. Vincent's sense of loss redoubled. Now she was truly gone, and he huddled by the headstone of her grave. Crystalline droplets rained from him. His heart contorted in the agony of this second loss. Grief tore through him and made him oblivious to all else. There was nothing but the agonizing torture of his distress—the shattering of his self.

35

Vincent looked up at the moon, still high in the heavens. *How can she be so tranquil? How does none of this pain and suffering affect her? She just is.* He sat up and looked about. He felt drained. There was nothing left within him. The shattered slivers of his heart littered the bottom of his chest cavity. His cup of grief was empty. *How can I ever love again? How will I ever be me again?* His thoughts brought aches to his chest. Breathing was painful, but the discomfort was numbed by his overall frame of mind. Nothing was good, and nothing could ever be right again.

When he rose to his feet, he glanced around the clearing. Everything came to a grinding halt. He trembled, but his mind remained unmodelled clay. A shadowy figure sat upon the log to one side of the clearing. Vincent shut his eyes and opened them again in slow trepidation. The figure still hunched over in the darkened shadows.

Vincent's mutilated heart leapt into his throat, hammering for release from within his body. He swallowed, but knew he could not make a sound. Terror rampaged through him, paralysing his whole being. He backed into the rock once more, but there was no comfort. Gisela would not save him this time. She was gone. His heart clenched. With eyes watering, he clutched his chest. The next iron-fisted contraction followed hard on the heels of the first. He rang for a breath, eyes straining against the confines of this physical agony. He tried to bring air into his lungs with fast, shallow inhalations, but the metal bands confining his ribcage compressed everything. Vincent collapsed to his knees.

A touch jolted him back out of his physical disintegration. Soothing kindness enveloped him, and Vincent saw a man in a voluminous robe steady him. "There, there," the person consoled. His voice was deep, and his pale green eyes exuded calm. "Breathe," the firm tenor instructed. The man's timbre rumbled through Vincent. It was a resonance for calm and Vincent did as instructed. Sweet air flowed into his starved lungs, sweeping away the anxiety gripping him a heartbeat before.

"You have had a rough night, but all will be well. They have gone and won't return."

Vincent's mind struggled to grasp this information.

It bounced around his brain without being taken up. Equally unfathomable was the unusual appearance of his companion. The man's billowing robes were made of homespun, dyed a deep blue. His flaxen hair was long, far longer than customary for men of Vendale. He had a round face with smooth, pale cheeks.

The cogs in Vincent's mind whirred back to life—the spinning teeth grabbing each other to achieve coherence once more. *Elf. Guardian of the forest.* He searched his memory. What did he even know about these creatures? *Very little*, he had to admit to himself. They were reclusive. He became aware of the elf muttering to himself and tuned in to what this unknown creature was doing. The elf's brows were knitted in a tight frown, and he shuffled about the mound of semi-compacted earth on which Vincent still stood.

"So much waste," the elf rumbled. He shook his head, cast about some more. Then he began to weave his hands about in the air.

Vincent observed in wide-eyed wonder and felt the oppressive heaviness that hung about him dissipate. Breathing became easier. Lightness filled his being once more.

When the elf dropped his hands back to his sides, Vincent felt released. "What did you do?"

The elf glanced up, his expression piercing. Then a soft smile spread across his features, calming the ice in his eyes. "I released the wiley magic from this place."

"Wiley?" Vincent's brow arched.

"The ghosts you met earlier. Wileys are the spirits of female humans filled with anger and hate. Their core magic allows them to remain on this plane in spectral form."

"Magic? But they were all peasants."

A hearty guffaw spilled from the elf. "You humans are so funny. Magic is a state of being that humans and elves have access to. Social status has nothing to do with it. What an odd notion."

Vincent paused to process, then whispered, "So, Gisela had magic?" Once the question was vocalised, the stupidity of his ignorance hit him hard. *Of course she was a magic user!* Hadn't he seen her transform into a phoenix? Not even an hour before she'd protected him with a gleaming shield of light. Vincent lowered his gaze. *Obvious!* Then a thought struck him, and he caught the elf's eye. "What happened to her? She didn't disappear like the others. It felt like she was snuffed out, gone forever."

The elf nodded. "Yes. The new one, she passed on. She exhausted her magic and couldn't keep herself on this plane." He paused, lost in thought. "Although," the elf continued, "from what I can sense, she wasn't a proper wiley anyway. She would have passed over sooner or later whether she used her magic or not. She was not tied here by hate or resentment."

Vincent nodded. "No, she held no animosity. Gisela was something else." His mind wandered, and he thought back to the scene where she'd protected him and held off the ghostly horde. "Why did the... wileys... want to harm me?" he stumbled over the unusual word. "I never did anything to them."

Pale hair swung from side to side as the elf shook his head. His eyes held a deep sadness. "They are filled with loathing of all men. They believe they were wronged in life and refuse to let go their hatred. It is why they roam this plane and exact revenge from any human men who cross their path. The wileys use their magic and the vibrations of nature to ensnare their victims. Be grateful for the young lady who kept you from their grasp. She saved your life."

Vincent shifted. He knew it was true. After a brief pause for reflection, he added, "You say vibrations of nature. I heard a beautiful music that sounded like the mountains and the forest all resonating in harmony. What was that?"

"You heard it?" the elf's eyebrows disappeared into his hair. "You are more in tune than I thought." He smiled at Vincent, then continued. "Yes, that is the natural magical vibration of all that is. It expresses as music to our ears. It is a very lucky thing to hear it. I have never heard of such a thing, a human male being able to detect the higher resonance of magic. That is a true gift from the higher energies."

Silence stretched between them as they contemplated this anomaly. Then Vincent's mind pounced on another thought. "Is the magic the reason why Gisela was such an exceptional dancer?"

"Exceptional is the key word there." The elf bobbed his head as he gazed off into the distance. With a start, he returned to the present and added arms waving to illustrate grandeur, "Exceptional cook, exceptional weaver, exceptional healer... even exceptional mother. They illustrate their magic through their larger-than-life achievements in the everyday."

The elf turned away, then stopped as if struck by a thought. He pivoted and graced Vincent with a humorous smile. "It's been a pleasure making your acquaintance, human." He bobbed his head, then added in a more serious tone, "I must be on my way. I have several more spots to clear of latent magic before the sun rises, and you humans start prancing about."

Vincent tilted his head. "Was that the weaving you did with your hands?"

"Yes," came the reply. "As guardians of the natural world, it is our duty to ensure the magic is harmonious. When things get out of balance, that is where the real trouble starts."

He raised a hand in farewell and slipped between the trees. Vincent was awed by how silent the elf's motions were. Not a single leaf crackled under his feet. He watched the blue-clad figure disappear from view beyond the trees.

It is time, he thought. *Time to go back.*

36

Vincent hurried towards Ylvaton. There were two reasons for his haste. He hoped speed would warm up his body to fend off the chill caused by the bone-aching cold just before dawn. He also knew his people would be looking for him and wanted to allay their fears as soon as possible.

Sure enough, when he reached the town, every house had a candle flickering, and people milled about on the streets. Flaming torches cast unsteady light into the darkened alleys. The villagers shouted and called. As soon as Vincent stepped into sight, a horde converged on him and chaperoned him back in the direction of the inn at the centre of Ylvaton.

Fred, his bodyguard, rushed forward when he saw the gathering crowd head to the inn. Vincent noted Fred's approach and felt guilt constricting his throat at the wide-eyed way the tough man cast about, searching. Vincent grabbed Fred's shoulders to still his rising panic. Holding him in a firm grip, Vincent said, "I was not myself yesterday. I ran off without thinking. I apologise. It won't happen again." The heavy, muscular man closed his eyes and breathed. Then he met Vincent's gaze, nodded and followed one pace behind his prince.

Oskar was not so easily appeased. When Vincent's friend caught sight of him he flared up in a rant, "Vincent Edward Rupert Louis Venador—" there was a collective gasp from the crowd. Every commoner who ushered Vincent towards the inn took a step away from him and dropped their gazes while Oskar continued with his diatribe. "If you ever do something like this to me again, I swear, on my mother's name, I will tell your royal father so he may have you whipped. It wouldn't surprise me if all the hairs on my head have turned white because of you!"

Vincent struggled to hold back the laughter bubbling up inside him. He succeeded, but couldn't suppress a grin from spreading wide, splitting his visage with his amusement. "I suppose you'll just make the most of the experience gained, *old* friend."

Oskar's brow rippled into a series of deep gullies. He huffed. Glaring lightning sparks at Vincent, he folded his arms over his chest. Then he hesitated. The gleam in his eyes lightened, and within moments, a loud guffaw echoed into the night. Oskar clapped his friend on the back, jostling him as he did so, and then they strode back to the Golden Boar Inn, laughing together.

By mid-morning, the village was once again bustling and full of motion. No one had slept much that night what with the disappearance of the town's favourite aristocrat who turned out to be none other than their crown prince. For a full generation, the villagers recounted events and told time in relation to the prince's visit. His birthday even became a specially celebrated holiday in Ylvaton for the people were so enamoured of the man who came among them as one of them and loved a girl from their village that they felt a strong bond with their future king.

Vincent was given a hearty send-off, and he glanced back many times as his horse took him further and further away from the place where his heart was enchanted and the uncertain, feeble young man he'd been, swept away. His thoughts lingered on the woman who had turned everything he knew on its head and provided him with gifts far greater than any he'd ever received before. With his back straight and his spirits high, Vincent took note of the ideas whirring in his mind.

The elf he'd met in the forest had provided a number of thoughts to work through, and while he rode towards the high mountains of his home, his mind began slotting the pieces of a grand plan into place. He remembered his mother complaining of her magic students' mediocrity. He recalled the force of the magic Gisela wielded, the sheer power of her being, which she poured out into her dancing. Recalling the elf's disdain for human social hierarchy, Vincent struck on a thought. *What if the aristocracy is losing magical power because of inbreeding? What if the bloodlines of the royal mages' circle can be renewed? How can such a thing be done?*

His mind kept firing questions and even some ideas, but Vincent knew he would never be able to convince his mother to allow commoners to be trained in magic. *That won't work. She'll say it's impossible and dangerous. But what will work?* As he mulled over these thoughts, something else rose to the fore. The realisation was unrelated, but equally important to him.

I cannot marry Catherine, he admitted to himself. *I do not love her, and we will only cause each other suffering. I love Gisela, and marrying anyone I don't love would be a desecration of everything Gisela taught me. I cannot treat her memory so poorly.* But how could he make his parents see reason? They would insist on tradition, on Catherine's honour and her family's. *I have to get out of it somehow,* he determined. *They cannot expect to rule my life anymore. I am master of my own destiny, and I shall choose whom I marry. They cannot force me, and I must stand by what is right.* He thought about it more, and although he twisted the situation and tried to observe it from every side, he struggled to find a satisfactory solution. He even wondered what Gisela might have counselled, but it didn't help him gain clarity on how to approach the subject with his parents, or even Catherine.

The day was balmy and warm for the autumn. Vincent broke away from his thoughts and rode to catch up with Oskar. For once, he enjoyed his friend's boisterous nature and laughed at Oskar's account of the evening before and the frantic search he and the folk of Ylvaton embarked on. Vincent did not confide in his friend the experience with the wileys and his final encounter with Gisela. He found it hard enough to believe—and he'd lived it. Vincent knew his friend could not understand the deeply moving incident and how it ignited Vincent's appreciation for a more spiritual perception of the world.

When evening fell, the party stopped at a roadside inn, and Vincent retired. Sleep claimed him the instant he fell back into the mattress. There was no resisting what he'd held at bay the entire day. He slept without dreams or interruption for the whole night, waking rested and refreshed at dawn.

Rousing his companions, he met bleary-eyed questioning with a firm order. "We leave in an hour. It is time to return to Realtown and my duties at the palace." One or two yawns were stifled, but the eye-rubbing and grumbling was not. Vincent recognised the signs of fatigue in his companions and decided to encourage them. "If we leave early, we can make it to the palace before nightfall. You will sleep in your own beds tonight. And think of the feast you'll receive after our long absence."

A cheer went up, and he smiled to himself. *That was well done. Uncharacteristic, too.* He nodded and headed to the inn's common room for his breakfast. *I am growing,* he thought. *I am a better man today than I was yesterday. That should please Father.*

Vincent was in high spirits throughout the day. His reflection on magic and the opportunity to do good for his country emboldened him. The knowledge that he dared do things he'd always been too afraid to do before made his heart float. Memories of his beloved Gisela, though tinged with sadness, filled him with love and contentment. Her blessing was a constant companion now.

He thought about her parting words and as his gaze drifted up the sheer crags that raised their walls into the bright sky, he whispered, "I, for one, did receive your message, dearest, and I'll see the love and peace you blessed me with brought to this realm."

In the afternoon, clouds drifted overhead, and he was grateful his company was spared rainfall on their last day of travel. The sky was streaked with fingers of pink when he rode over the drawbridge to the clattering beat of hoof-falls. His gaze was drawn to the majestic marble stag. *Regal,* he thought. *Like I must be. Like I shall be henceforth.* He heard the sweet tinkling of water flowing from the rim of the fountain into the carved bowl below. The sound of life lent his heart wings and he soared up to where bright pennants fluttered in the breeze.

Gisela, he thought. *How I would have loved to bring you here. It is so beautiful with the mountains.* He was home. Life was beautiful—worth living. And he would make the most of everything he had.

EPILOGUE

Vincent strode through the tall, carved, wooden doors into his father's apartments. His eyes appraised the band of carved panels and he saluted the glorious achievements of his forebears. *One day,* he promised himself, *the adventure of Vincent and the wileys will also grace this hall.* Holding his shoulders back, he strode forward with determination. Gone were the days of doubt and self-criticism. *It is my time now, and I am worthy.*

A movement called upon his attention from the corner of his eye. He observed his father. The king sat behind his desk, writing with an eagle's speed. The nib of his quill scratched over the parchment, but Vincent studied the man for the first time in many years. What he saw was an overweight man of middling years. His jowls sagged like empty bags. His face was framed by obsidian hair which was longer than he ever remembered his father allowing it to grow. It hung just over the tops of the king's ears. He seemed drawn, and his skin was waxen. Pearly beads of sweat dotted his forehead, and every so often he would rub his hand over his left breast as though alleviating discomfort. The king wore a set of matching coat and breeches of deepest violet with silver patterns embroidered on the fabric. Ermine trimming added another ostentatious touch to the ensemble. Vincent shuddered at the thought of the expense and how pointless he knew all the posturing was. *When my time comes, I'll show that it is possible to maintain appearances without bankrupting the treasury.*

He held his own council though and waited for his father to finish with his business. The familiar hard, brown eyes raised to look up at him. A part of Vincent quailed in memory of his usual response to the king's gaze, but his new self pushed aside the trembling, undecided youth he'd been before his journey. Like always, his father said nothing and Vincent smiled at the ease with which patience came to him now. The king stood and faced his son, a disapproving look twitching his greying eyebrows together.

"So, you've finished gallivanting over the countryside."

It was a statement more than a question, and Vincent decided to speak before his father could let loose his disdain. "Yes, Father. I took the time I needed for reflection and to learn what needed to be learned. I am satisfied now. I know my worth and can serve the people as they deserve. I shall take on the duties you suggested I assume last spring, and which I foolishly rejected because I didn't understand their importance." He paused. When he saw his father's raised eyebrow and mouth hanging open, Vincent continued. "I also made a discovery during my travels. I would like to discuss it with you in greater depth. It is about magic and how it may be possible to renew the magical powers in the Royal Circle of Mages. I suppose we can discuss it together with Mother over the coming days."

The king grunted, and his eyebrows drew together in a v. "It is not our place to meddle with the mages. They deal with magic, and we deal with everything else."

"If that is what you believe is best for the country, then I have nothing further to say on the matter," Vincent forced out through clenched jaws. *I'll at least mention it to Mother. If she doesn't think it important, then it can remain my pet project until I take over the throne.*

He made ready to leave, but his father stopped him. "I shall remind you of your promise. Before you left, you agreed to announce your engagement."

Vincent's stomach clenched, but he schooled his features and replied as lightly as he could, "I thought my upcoming birthday ball would be an adequate occasion to make an announcement of that magnitude."

Before the king could offer his blessing or derision,

Vincent spun around and strode out of the room. *That was stupid!* he berated himself. *I should have told him right away I have no intention of marrying Catherine. I had better hurry up and find someone suitable to replace her with before the ball, otherwise they'll force me into this awful union. I should have been firmer.* He took a deep breath. *Well, it is done now. I must make the best of it instead.*

He calmed and hurried to his mother's quarters. Vincent met his tall, thin mother in her antechamber. She reclined on a chaise longue and perused a book. Silver streaks infiltrated the dark ebony of her tresses. Deep lines tugged at the corners of her mouth and between her eyebrows. Vincent only noted a few around her eyes. *She's far too stressed*, he thought. *Hardly ever smiles.*

"Mother," Vincent strode forward, arms outstretched, "I have returned in good health, as you can see. I have learned much and feel rejuvenated."

"Ah, Vincent, my boy!" she exclaimed, snapping the book shut and rising. She embraced him, adding, "You've been gone so long! I've missed you."

Vincent nodded and smiled. "I learned many things, mother. It was a good journey, and I know I can make a difference."

"Oh, that's nice," she said, patting his hand. "You must be famished! Look at how thin you've grown. How could you leave me all these months?" She linked her arm in his and pulled him out into the hallway. "Come, Catherine is sure to want to see you."

Vincent doubted it, but knew he couldn't get out of Catherine's company quite as easily as he'd hoped. He noticed he was biting his bottom lip and stopped. With two breaths, he returned to the state of calm he recognised as his own state of being. *Another opportunity to talk about magic will surely arise. It is probably best to wait for a good moment to broach the subject with her.*

With that thought, Vincent entered the dining hall. A squeal assaulted his ears, and next he knew, a ball of energy had hurtled across the room and embraced him in a stifling hug. "You're back!" Madeleine breathed. "You must tell me all about it."

"Madeleine," the queen reprimanded with more than a hint of disapproval, "that is no way for a young countess to behave. You should be ashamed of yourself."

Allowing her arms to fall to her sides, Madeleine stepped back, shoulders slumped and a sheepish pout contorting her usually joyful features. Her raven hair was pinned up on her head in a series of swooping whorls, and Vincent smiled at her, hoping he could perk her spirits back up again. He winked and mouthed, "I'll tell you all about it tomorrow."

THE END

Gisela's Passion may be at an end, but the journey does not end here...

The Siblings' Tale is a two-part series set a few decades after the circumstances set out in Gisela's Passion and follows the consequences of Vincent's chance discovery in the woods one autumn night. Further fairy tale retellings will also be forthcoming in the Elisabeth and Edvard's World series. Subscribe to

Astrid's monthly newsletter to stay up to date with those upcoming releases.

And don't miss THE WISHMASTER SERIES, coming 2020, where you'll get to meet the wandering storyteller Viola Alerion and join her on her amazing journey, accompanied by her apprentice.

Subscribe to Astrid's newsletter at https://www.subscribepage.com/subscribeE+EWORLD

ACKNOWLEDGMENTS

This novel owes its existence to many, many people. Firstly, I would like to thank my sister Theresa. Your love for dancing, and your choice to make your passion your career is something I will always treasure. I know how hard that decision was for you, and I am eternally grateful you decided to go for what you love. Thank you for all your help giving Gisela that dancer's spark and helping me with fun turns of phrases to give this book that extra twist, just for lovers of dance. Also, thank you for dragging me to all those ballet performances, keeping my love for the art alive so I could share that with my readers now.

To my "familia política", thank you. Thank you for taking me in as one of your own and giving me an extra family. To Kyndes, I am eternally grateful for your unwavering support to my growing family and for showing me what is possible with all the amazing things that you do. Ámbar-Maya and Aliosha, thank you for being my extra siblings. Your support means the world to me. Mamá Teté, thank you for the time spent teaching me Spanish. Thank you for taking me in and always showering me with your love, and thank you for letting me get to know your darling Alexandra whom I never had the opportunity to meet. I know talking of her is hard for you, and I appreciate you going through that pain for me. Although I didn't know it at the time, it became very important as I wrote this book. To everyone else from the Nuñez de León and Johnsson families, I say thank you.

My uncle Verdun, without your generous contribution on a joyful occasion many years ago, I would never have had the opportunity to visit Peru. Your support, unwittingly, made this book and the whole kingdom of Vendale possible. Thank you for your generosity and support that sparked the wings of my imagination.

To my book-angels, Qat and Emily, I could not do this without you. Your work is every bit as meaningful as mine, and I am grateful for all the expertise you infuse into my book-babies. Thank you for your time and your dedication. It is always a pleasure working with you.

Amanda Strydom, songsmith of my heart who writes music for my soul. Thank you for all your years of dedicated work that inspires me every day. Thank you for your music, which has influenced me so much, that even phrases from your song, *Scattered Thunder*, make for the perfect titles of this book's two sections. Your songs are a light (and darkness) in my life, and for that I am truly grateful.

I also lavish gratitude on a great friend and supporter, Julie Soper. Thank you for all your advice, support and feedback. You always give me just the push I need to make things even better. I admire you and love that we encourage and inspire each other. You are simply the best! Thanks also go to Ilona Nurmela, Dr Rebecca Verghese and Rose Flynn for your incredible attention to detail, support and advice. Thank you, my friends.

Anne, you are the best mother I could ever have wished for. Thank you for supporting me and my sisters in our passions, for being our role model by going after what you love and in so doing, guiding the way for us to do the same. Thank you for sparking my love of books and Theresa's love for dance. Thank you for all the interminable hours spent taking us to performances, rehearsals and concerts. I loved every moment of it and my love for Giselle was definitely sparked by your dedication. Thank you for bending over backwards to make my eighteenth birthday so special and taking me and my friends to see Giselle, which at the time was my favourite ballet.

Last, but only because you're the most important, Renato, thank you. Thank you for everything. You support every endevour I ever embark on and not once do you doubt I can pull it off. You're always there to catch me when I flounder and to push me when I want to put things off. I am grateful for everything you do so I can take time to write, edit, and market my books. Thank you for being you and always having my back. Thank you for all these years you've been by my side, my rock, my sanity and my perfect match.

ABOUT THE AUTHOR

Astrid Vogel de Johnsson is a South African author and anthropologist now residing in Sweden. In early childhood, she showed an interest in reading and languages—interests which her family encouraged. Astrid started writing her first novel at age 12 and now writes high fantasy, exploring her passion for cultures and languages. She is fluent in five European languages. She is happily married with two adorable children. When she isn't writing, Astrid likes to read, take walks in nature, play silly games with her children, do embroidery, and play music.

BOOKS BY ASTRID V.J.

Elisabeth and Edvard's World (published)

Gisela's Passion

Aspiring, Part 1 of the Siblings' Tale

Becoming, Part 2 of the Siblings' Tale

The Wishmaster Series (forthcoming 2020)

The Apprentice Storyteller

Becoming Spellwright

Master Wordmage

Made in the USA
San Bernardino, CA
23 January 2020